Julia Jones

The Teenage Years

Book 2

Roller Coaster Love

Katrina Kahler

Table of Contents

Evil...

Her blue eyes stared into mine. The look of hatred was so intense, it cut through me like a knife.

I could see her lips moving. She seemed to be yelling at me, spitting the words in my face. For some strange reason though, I could not hear a thing. The eerie silence as I frantically tried to move out of her reach, made the whole scene surreal, as though it wasn't really happening.

But even in my dazed state, I was sure she was there, only inches away, menacing and threatening; the look of loathing clear in her features! And it was in slow motion that I watched her raised hand drop. I followed its arc, almost graceful in its approach and I knew with certainty, it would reach its mark.

Without warning, I saw something glint. What was in her grasp? What was the sharp object she was holding with such fierce intensity and aiming with deadly accuracy at my face?

With horror, I gaped at the gleaming blade. It had caught a flicker of light from an overhanging bulb, causing it to glow once more. Numb with fear I stood, riveted to my spot against the wall, unable to move.

What was wrong with me? Why couldn't I get out of her way? I tried to lift one leg and then the other. It was then I found that I was frozen into place, a motionless form at the mercy of the devil.

Abruptly, the silence broke; deathly, blood-curdling sounds that filled me with dread.

But who was screaming? Who was making that terrible noise? Flicking my eyes from side to side, I tried to focus on the scene around me. Nothing seemed familiar. What was this place? What was I doing, glued to the wall? And worse still…where had she gone?

"Julia! Julia! Julia, are you okay?"

"What happened, Julia? Did you faint? Should I call an ambulance? Julia, answer me!"

The voices around me were a blur and as I stared at the vaguely familiar faces, I tried to shake my mind back into focus. Then with an abrupt movement, I shoved the hovering figures out of the way and staggered shakily to my feet. I had to reach the bathroom, I could see it within view down the hallway but I knew I only had seconds to spare. My head spun in a dizzy fog as nausea rose to the back of my throat. Clasping my hand firmly over my mouth, I stumbled towards the closed door and frantically pushed it open.

"Julia, are you okay?"

"Julia, can we help you?"

The voices echoed outside the cubicle and when I finally emerged, drenched with sweat and ghostly white, the look of concern on their faces was genuine.

Sitting me carefully down in a chair that had been propped in the corner, the girls then proceeded to use some damp toweling to sponge my forehead. I leaned my head back against the wall. Taking in deep breaths of air until with huge relief, I gradually began to feel better.

"We need to get you home, Julia! You've obviously come

down with some type of terrible stomach bug. You should probably see a doctor!"

"We found you on the floor; it looked as though you were hallucinating. You were saying the weirdest things. We couldn't understand a word."

I looked at the two faces staring into my own. I just wanted to go home, climb into bed and sleep forever.

What is going on???...

Sitting up with a start, I glanced around at my surroundings and realized that I was in my own bed and it had turned dark outside. Several hours must have passed since I arrived home. I recalled roughly forcing open the front door and feeling intense relief to find the house silent and empty. I didn't want to face anyone and climbed the stairs to my room, desperate to close the door behind me and shut out the world.

As I lay there, groggy with sleep, the day's events gradually came flooding back and I considered the roller coaster of emotions I was overcome with from the moment I opened my locker.

But had I imagined it all? Had it all simply been a dream of sorts, a figment of my imagination? Or a reaction to some terrible stomach bug just as the girls had suggested?

Then the image of the voodoo doll appeared sharply in my head. NO! I had definitely not imagined that. It was real. I clearly remembered ripping out the needles and any other random bits that I could tear away. Then I threw the entire contents into the nearest trash can. I had wanted it out of my sight, forever dismantled and banished to oblivion.

That was right after...right after what? I clawed through my memory banks, hoping to remember.

Was Sara there? Had there actually been a knife? That part was the foggiest of all and I struggled to recall the details, unsure as to what had really gone on. Perhaps it was some kind of hallucination, a crazed state of mind that had tumbled into overdrive, bringing my darkest fears to life.

The moments afterward were clear though, and I was so grateful those girls had been there and offered to take me home. They were seniors who I'd met at one time in the library and who happened to strike up a welcoming conversation. On numerous occasions since I'd come across them on the school grounds and they were always very friendly.

It had been a pure stroke of luck that they'd returned to their own lockers before heading home for the weekend. They'd had to retrieve a forgotten textbook, one that was needed for an assignment they were working on together; but that was the reason they found me lying lifeless on the hallway floor. By that stage, the area was pretty much deserted, so it was extremely fortunate that they appeared.

Acting on impulse, I quickly hopped out of bed and reached for my laptop. When I turned it on, the start button glowed brightly in the darkened room. If my mom was at home I certainly did not want her knowing I was awake. So I sat in the darkness on my bed, waiting for my computer to start. I was definitely not in the mood for her incessant chatter which I was sure I'd be forced to listen to, and right then, I did not want to discuss the nightmare I had woken up from, not with her anyway.

"How was your day, Julia?" I quietly mimicked her voice, the tone identical to hers.

"Well, Mom, if you really want to know…I found a voodoo doll shoved into my locker and then I kind of hallucinated and was later found passed out on the hallway floor. But anyway, how was *your* day??"

Her initial look of shock would be followed by a small laugh at the absurdity of my response. She would shake her head with the assumption I was sharing some random joke, one that she had no understanding of. She'd then simply continue on with an overview of her own day, which I really wasn't interested in hearing about. Regardless, she was the last person I would even consider sharing my latest drama with.

I was also aware that I'd missed dinner, something she'd be sure to mention, but food was the last thing on my mind right then.

As soon as the Google homepage appeared, I typed the words, voodoo doll into the search bar. To begin with, all I could find were the lyrics of a song with the same name but after some more searching, I located some information.

However, it was not what I had expected.

Apparently, the original purpose of voodoo dolls was to manifest positive feelings and intentions. The belief was that feelings such as love, happiness joy, and good karma could be created. But after some further reading, I also found that if the dolls were used for bad intentions or with the purpose of hurting others, then this would create a karmic backlash with the creator becoming the one to receive the negative energy.

Wild thoughts raced through my mind as I closed down the computer and reflected on what I had just read. Had my physical and mental state been a reaction to the doll that was hidden in my locker? Or, had I simply been suffering from some terrible stomach bug, possibly even food poisoning from something I'd bought at the canteen? I knew that food poisoning could definitely create terrible symptoms; maybe that was what caused me to become so ill. Surely there had to be a logical explanation.

Even if that were the case, whoever was responsible for the

hideous looking object that had been created to resemble me, deserved whatever repercussions came to them! It was all probably just some hocus-pocus but to even consider doing something so vile, was beyond me. It was incredible that a person could stoop that low in order to play a stupid prank.

Visions of Sara's evil glare appeared in my head once more. I was certain she was responsible. Who else would have done such a thing? The more I thought about it, the more convinced I was that she was the culprit. It all reeked of Sara.

I remembered the time she locked me in an isolated cabin in the middle of the night. It was during our grade seven camp and I was absolutely terrified. Especially after a sliver of thick glass had sliced through my hand as I tried to escape out the only window. So many years later, I could still picture the blood; within seconds it had totally covered my hand. That was just before I passed out, the fear of bleeding to death in the middle of the thick bushland, too much to cope with.

Yes, I was totally convinced that Sara was capable of anything.

What worried me most though was the idea of facing her at school the following day. And as well as that, it seemed that her ruthless ability for scaring others was limitless. If she could follow through with a scenario as crazy as a voodoo doll, what else did she have in store?

As I stared out the window towards the night sky, I took no comfort at all in the full moon that was beaming its pool of bright light onto the floor beside my bed. Turning away, I screwed my eyes tightly closed, wanting to shut out any and all sensations that threatened to invade my subconscious. But still, the sinister fear I was trying to evade, trickled silently down my spine. I could feel it, a sneaking, invasion of my mind and body, creeping right through to my soul.

Nausea formed in the pit of my stomach and I knew beyond doubt, it was not a stomach bug that was causing it. Gripping tightly to the sheets, I pulled them firmly to my chin, almost like a shield of protection.

If only it were that easy. The thought was clear in my head as a loud and resentful sigh escaped my lips.

The last thing I remember before finally drifting into a troubled sleep was Blake's smiling face flashing through my thoughts. But it was quickly ripped away a fraction of a second later and abruptly replaced with menacing eyes and an evil stare.

The eyes were a vivid blue, piercing and familiar.

Even though long blond hair framed the face. I was certain it was the face of the devil.

Distraught...

The days that followed, passed by in a cloudy haze. Sara had not been seen at school all week and although I was thankful for her absence, I felt an uneasy reprieve, convinced that it would not last.

No one seemed aware of the incident that had occurred in the hallway by the lockers. Well, no one spoke of it so I figured it had gone unnoticed; except by the two senior girls who had helped me that was.

"Are you feeling better now, Julia?" one had asked the following day when I bumped into her during lunch break, the concern still evident on her face.

"I'm so much better now, thanks, Maxine!" I smiled. "And thanks heaps again for the ride home! I don't know what I would have done if you girls hadn't found me!"

We chatted some more and that had been the end of the conversation. Incident over and done with and never to be heard of or spoken of again. Or so it appeared. And I was extremely grateful to put it all behind me. It certainly wasn't something that I wanted to become public knowledge. I was just glad that the area was deserted at the time. I also figured that I must have imagined the image of Sara with a knife. Perhaps it actually had been some kind of hallucination. After all, I was quite ill with a terrible fever so who knows what tricks my mind was playing on me.

The week flew by quickly and true to my word, I did my best to avoid Blake. I'd convinced myself that for his sake and my own, we needed to move on. Although I sensed him staring in my direction several times in class, any time I noticed him nearby I put my head down or tuned my back, making sure the message was clear.

I wanted nothing to do with him.

So why was I feeling so miserable? Overwhelmed with a sense of loss, I could barely concentrate on my schoolwork or anything else for that matter.

"We're destined to be together!" Blake had once said, back when we were in middle school.

But we were just kids then. What did we know! And besides that, too much had changed. Regardless of how miserable I felt, I could not come to terms with the fact that in my absence, he had fallen for Sara. After all we'd been through in the past, how could he even have considered it? I was sure that was what hurt the most and I had no idea how to put it behind me. As well as that, Sara's menacing stare was too fresh in my mind and I knew that while she was around, a relationship between Blake and I could never work.

Forcing myself to clear away all thoughts of Blake and Sara and the recent locker scene that continued to creep to the forefront of my mind, I focused on the weekend ahead. Images of my dad came to mind and the corners of my mouth automatically curved into a smile. He was due to arrive home that night and I was convinced that everything would return to normal once he returned, even if it was only for the weekend.

Fleetingly, I then thought of Barry, the over-friendly tradesman my mother was so besotted with. The very idea of him caused my skin to crawl. Having Dad back would solve that problem though. His return that evening was the key and I pictured his smiling face as he walked into the house. I'd planned to cook his favorite meal and had given

Mom a shopping list with the ingredients I needed. I just hoped she'd remember to get everything I asked for as I really wanted our family dinner to be special.

When I entered the house later that afternoon, it was the best I had felt all week and I was keen to get started. I knew that I'd need quite a bit of time for preparation but I only had a couple of hours to spare before Dad arrived home. As I entered the kitchen, however, I was struck with a vision that was utterly unexpected. What on earth was Barry doing in our house? It was the night that Dad was due back and there was the tradesman, the one who I despised, sitting comfortably at our kitchen table chatting easily with my mother.

I eyed the bags of groceries still sitting unpacked on the benchtop and then looked questioningly in her direction.

"Julia!" she exclaimed. "You're home! I have some bad news, darling and I know that you'll be terribly disappointed."

Instantly my stomach filled with dread. "What is it? Has something happened to Dad?"

"No, no, nothing like that," she said in a soothing voice that I found frustratingly irritating. "Your father rang about an hour ago to say that there's been an emergency in the office and he's the only one who can deal with it, so he's been asked to stay behind."

"What?? You mean he's not coming home tonight?" I already knew the answer to my question, but I had to ask it anyway.

All she could do was look at me, something akin to sympathy showing in her expression. But she was unable to respond. Not that she needed to. It was clear that I wouldn't be seeing my dad that weekend.

Then I glanced at Barry, who I hadn't even acknowledged until that moment.

"So what's he doing here?" The words were out of my mouth before I could stop them and I had been unable to control the rude tone that betrayed my contempt at seeing him sitting so comfortably in our kitchen.

"Julia, I know you're disappointed about your dad not coming come home but that is no excuse for rudeness. Show some respect, young lady!"

I glared at her with contempt. I hated her and I hated the man beside her. The two of them sickened me. How could she sit there in such a contented manner while that creepy jerk sat in my father's favorite chair? And all the while, my dad was working his butt off in some miserable place all on his own!

Tears formed in the corners of my eyes and I blinked several times, furiously trying to fight them off. I did not want to give my mother or Barry the satisfaction of seeing me upset. Without another word, I turned away and raced up the stairs to my room, anxious to escape their presence. Slamming the door shut behind me, I threw myself down onto the quilted cover of my bed and buried my face in the pillow. The sobs wracked my body and I was unable to stop.

Distraught with disappointment and despair, I continued to sob. Why was my life such a mess? How had I come to a point where everything had gone so wrong? The pounding inside my head worsened until it threatened to explode and I tried to choke back the endless stream of tears that were drenching my pillow.

I hate her! I hate her! I hate her!

The words raced around and around in my thoughts until, in total frustration, I voiced what I was no longer able to contain.

"I hate youuuuuuuuu!!!!!"

Screaming loudly at the closed door, I waited for her response. But there was none. No reaction whatsoever.

In frustration, I picked up a shoe that I had kicked off earlier and hurled it at the door, only to watch it fall uselessly to the floor. It didn't even make a dent in the paintwork, a total waste of energy.

When I felt a sudden vibration against my thigh, I realized my phone was ringing. Still in silent mode after keeping it hidden away in my pocket during class that afternoon, it buzzed loudly.

Overcoming the temptation to ignore it, I pulled it roughly from the lower pocket of my jacket and with a gasp, stared at the screen. The caller ID number that was flashing clearly was one I instantly recognized.

It was impossible not to know that number! It was still the same number it had always been and one I was sure I would always remember.

Tentatively, I clicked accept and slowly put the phone to my ear.

"Julia? It's me!"

Sitting silently on my bed, I was unable to reply.

"Julia, I know you're there! Please speak to me. I have to talk to you!"

The pleading in Blake's tone forced me to wipe the tears

from my eyes and murmur a quiet response. "What do you want?"

"I need to talk to you!"

I stared at the wall, the phone in my hand; the only sound I could hear was my shallow breathing.

"Julia, can I come over?"

"NO!" The abruptness of my response seemed to catch him off guard.

I heard his quick intake of breath. "I just thought…" he began.

"Thought what, Blake? That you could dump Sara and I'd instantly be there for you, just like that!"

"Of course not, I just…"

"Just what??" My angry retort sounded sharply into the phone, quickly cutting into the airwaves like a knife.

"I just want to talk, Julia. That's all." He was quiet then, no further response at all.

Instantly, I was filled with regret. Why was I being so mean? Why was I taking everything out on him? Surely, I could swallow my pride and listen to what he had to say.

I desperately wanted to share my feelings, the depth of my love for him, the love that lingered just below the surface, each day threatening to break my heart in two.

He spoke again, interrupting my thoughts. "I just want to say…I just want to say… I'm sorry."

An audible gasp escaped my lips. I had certainly not expected those words and while I waited quietly for him to continue, my head spun with emotion. Should I open up to him? What should I say in response? I was so afraid of being hurt.

I waited another moment, before finally opening my mouth to speak.

"Blake?"

But there was silence. Not another word came from the other end of the line.

"Blake?"

I repeated his name twice, three times, but it was no use. He was no longer there.

Staring at the reflection in my mirror on the wall opposite, I looked at myself with loathing, my eyes filling with tears once more. My life sucked and I had just made it a thousand times worse! Why couldn't I have just talked to him? What would be the harm in that? It was the perfect opportunity for us to make amends. Surely, I could just forget about Sara once and for all and stop adding to my misery!

Quickly, I grabbed the phone and pressed redial, watching nervously as his number lit up once more on the screen. I could feel my heart thumping wildly as I sat there waiting for him to pick up.

I didn't care about Sara or her stupid pranks. I needed to talk to Blake and right then, nothing else mattered.

Impatiently, I waited, the dial tone ringing loudly in my ear; until with a sinking dismay, I realized he was not going to answer.

I'd had my chance. He had come to me. But I turned him away.

Throwing my face into my pillow, I sobbed harder than ever.

If Only……

When my phone rang again sometime later, I fumbled clumsily, feeling through the folds of my quilt cover frantically trying to retrieve it before the tone rang out. Half asleep, I looked hopefully at the screen. Was it him calling me back? Was he trying once more in case I'd changed my mind?

Well, I had changed my mind. I did want to talk to him. He was the only one I'd ever really been able to talk to. And right then, I needed him more than ever!

Disappointed, I spoke into the phone. It wasn't him at all. It was one of the girls from school probably calling about another party we'd all been invited to. I'd originally planned to stay at home with my dad, but that plan had gone by the wayside.

"Hey," I said into the mouthpiece, trying to clear my throat and not sound as though I were still half asleep.

"Julia! You have to come to the party! It's going to be so good. Surely you can convince your dad to let you go!"

I smiled briefly at Lisa's enthusiasm. Although I really wasn't in the mood to be talking to her right then, she had the amazing ability to cheer people up. She continued on, her outgoing, infectious personality almost bursting through the phone.

I tried to refuse, explaining that I wasn't really feeling up to a party, but as usual, she was extremely persuasive; definitely a person who was very difficult to say no to.

However, I had a sneaking suspicion she was calling me because no one else was available. Beth was going away with her family for the weekend. Suzy had to go to her brother's college awards' ceremony and Jess was grounded because so far, her grades were way below average. So I figured that I was probably Lisa's last resort.

But I pushed those thoughts aside. In addition, it occurred to me that Blake might even be there. Feeling my pulse quicken at the thought of bumping into him, my decision was made; that thought alone was the spark I needed.

"Yeah, I'll go!" My quick reply caught her by surprise.

"Really?? Julia, that's so cool!! We'll have the best time!"

Excitedly, she continued on, "My mom said she'd drive me, so we can pick you up on the way. I'll be at your place in an hour."

Her response was all that was necessary to snap me out of the cloud of self-pity I'd been overwhelmed by. Then, as I ended the call, I considered one very tiny but important detail that I had completely overlooked. I hadn't even asked for my mom's permission.

Her face flashed into my mind and I could hear her words.

"What party?"

"And where is it being held?"

"Will there be parents at home?"

"And there had better not be any alcohol! I've heard terrible stories of teenage drinking at these parties!"

But I didn't care! I'd made up my mind and I was going to that party!

"Just let her try to stop me!" I muttered the words aloud as I flicked through my wardrobe, looking for something to wear.

My new blue skirt caught my eye. I'd bought it recently but hadn't worn it yet. It wasn't my usual style, much shorter and more fitted than I normally wore, but Beth had convinced me to buy it.

"Julia, it's perfect on you," she said enthusiastically when I tried it on during one of our shopping sprees not long ago. In the next instant, she also handed me a cute white midriff top that she persuaded me to purchase as well.

"You need some new clothes, Julia. And honestly, this outfit makes you look hot!"

Smiling, I recalled her words as I pulled the items from my cupboard and threw them onto the bed. I wasn't sure that what she had said was actually true, but the thought of her comment made me happy and I was so glad that I had something cool to wear.

Racing for the bathroom, I listened out for voices downstairs, half expecting to hear Barry and my mom still deep in animated conversation. But there were no sounds coming from downstairs at all. In fact, the house was eerily quiet.

Glimpsing a light shining from under my brother's bedroom door, I knocked before poking my head into his room. As usual, he was on his computer, headphones on and fully absorbed in the game on his screen. I found it hard to believe that he was in his senior year and still hooked on computer games.

Well, he obviously doesn't have a date tonight. The thought came to mind just as I asked him where our mother was.

Of course, he didn't hear me the first time and I had to yank his headphones off his ears to get his attention.

"What are doing?" he yelled angrily. "What's your problem?"

"Where's Mom?" I asked for the fourth time.

"She's gone to a movie!"

"With Barry?" I asked, shaking my head in disgust.

"I don't know. She said she'd be home late and there are leftovers in the fridge."

"Great!" I sighed, frowning at the thought of who she was probably out with. "If she comes home, can you tell her I'm staying at Lisa's tonight?"

My words fell on deaf ears. With his headphones back in place, he was once again engrossed in his game. A bomb could go off right outside his bedroom window and I was certain he'd still be oblivious to what was going on around him.

Rolling my eyes, I didn't bother repeating myself. I left his room and headed for the shower, keen to get moving so I'd be ready when Lisa arrived to pick me up. At least I didn't have to beg my mother for permission and I was grateful that at last, circumstances were working in my favor.

I climbed eagerly into the back of Lisa's mom's car shortly afterward and immediately sensed my friend's excitement. She turned from her spot in the front to say hello, and then discreetly indicated her bag that was on the floor next to my feet. Glancing inside, I spotted the flask that was partly hidden under her jacket. Grinning mischievously, she turned back towards the front to continue talking with her mom, who of course was ignorant to what her daughter was up to.

Unlike my mom and dad, Lisa's parents seemed to keep their cupboards well stocked with alcohol. Lisa had boasted several times at school that she'd been able to sneak away with what she wanted without them even realizing.

Laughing to myself, I contemplated the night ahead. However, I had no idea of what lay ahead for me.

Looking back, later on, I thought about the series of events that made my presence at the party even possible. I'd originally thought I would be at home with my family, my dad included, and if that had been the case, my night would have ended very differently.

If only my Dad had come home for the weekend…

If only I'd spoken to Blake on the phone and shared my true feelings…

If only I hadn't answered the phone when Lisa called…

If only my Mom had been around to prevent me from going out…

If only…

Terror…

I looked out the car window but all I could see was the blackness of the night. My instinct was telling me to open the door and run, to get as far away as possible. The problem was that I had no idea where we were. It was so dark and he had taken so many sharp turns.

My heart thumping, I dared to glance towards him. "Wh…where are we?" The words stammered from my mouth as I swallowed nervously. I could feel the beads of perspiration appearing on my brow while at the same time, an intensely sick feeling had formed in the pit of my stomach.

"Just relax," came the slurred reply.

"I want to go home! Please take me home!" My response was full of regret. Why had I agreed to a lift from this guy? I barely knew him. In fact, I had only just met him a few hours earlier. Hindsight was a wonderful thing, but right at that instant, it was no help whatsoever.

"It's okay, baby. Let's just chill here for a while!" His reply made me more uneasy and the knot in my stomach grew.

Gulping once more, I pleaded again. "I just want to go home!"

Sitting stiffly in my seat, my fingers on the handle of the door, I was ready to fling it open and run. But a rough hand jerked my shoulder back and before I could react, I was completely within his grasp.

His breath reeked of alcohol and when his unshaven face

nuzzled against my own as his hands groped my body, I thought I would throw up. The scene was surreal and I prayed that it was not really happening. Surely it was all part of a horrendous nightmare that I would wake up from at any minute.

Visions of the party we had left behind flooded my thoughts. Lisa had looked at me, eyebrows raised quizzically as I'd said a quick goodbye. At the time, I was desperate to leave. I had to get away and the offer of a ride home was the logical solution.

"Sure," I said eagerly, thinking it was a cool idea.

Of course, leaving the party with one of the hottest guys there would definitely attract attention. He was a senior named Joe Taylor and he was from another school. I knew that everyone would notice, but it was really only Blake who I was concerned with.

He had been flirting all night; except not with me. If Blake was trying to make me jealous, he had clearly succeeded. But I quickly decided that if he wanted to play that game, then I would too. And I wanted him to know it.

I was aware earlier on that Joe was interested in me. I could tell as soon as I caught him making eye contact from across the room.

"He's checking you out!" Lisa had said, nudging me discreetly with her elbow.

Embarrassed, I ignored her, and I also ignored the flirtatious looks Joe continued to direct my way. That was until he came over and stood by my side.

"I haven't seen you at any of these parties before!" he exclaimed. "Are you new in town?"

"Yeah, kind of!" I replied vaguely.

It didn't take long for us to strike up a friendly conversation and with Lisa's prompting, I even had a dance with him. He was a pretty cool dancer and it was fun. I was sure that the couple of drinks I'd had were helping to relax me though. Everything seemed so easy after a couple of drinks!

But then I spotted Blake across the room, his arm draped around some strange girl's shoulder whilst he cuddled up to her, the whole time, staring openly in my direction.

It was at that point, I knew I had to leave.

The rough feel of the unwanted hands on my body broke through my thoughts and with a sudden burst of strength, I pushed him away.

"Get off me!"

The words were abrupt, my message clear. I did not want any part of this. I hardly knew this guy. I had accepted his offer which was for a ride home, and that was all!

But he would not let me go. His grasp was insistent and his hands would not stop groping; under the hem of my dress, reaching along my thigh. Struggling, I tried to push him away.

It was then that his whole demeanor changed. He went from being a sloppy, disgusting drunk to someone else. Almost as though he were possessed, his hands became much rougher and much more persistent.

"Owww! Stop, you're hurting me!" His grasp on my arm

dug firmly into my flesh and when I saw the glint of serious aggression in his eyes, I knew that I was in trouble.

"I just want to go home," I pleaded once more.

Ignoring me, he stroked my leg and leaned in close, two moistened lips aiming directly for my own. The sudden feeling of revulsion created a rush of adrenaline and I shoved hard on the car door, forcing it open. He tightened his grip but with almost superhuman strength, I managed to break away.

My bag!

The thought struck me with fierce intensity and although I knew deep inside that I should just forget about it, there was no way I was going to leave my wallet with my money and ID card in his car.

Quickly reaching inside, I fumbled for the strap, thinking that I would grab it and run. I had no idea where I was but that was the last of my concerns. Then just as I was about to turn and race away into the safety of the darkness, there was a sharp tug on the loose ends of my long hair.

Why didn't I wear it up? Instantly, I was struck with the absurdity of my mistake.

My hair was hanging down the length of my back after having washed it earlier. I'd even made the effort to use my mom's hair straightener, which was something I rarely bothered with. I recalled thinking as I stood in front of the mirror, rushing to get ready, that just about every girl my age owns a hair straightener. But there I was, still using my mother's outdated device; so typical of my life.

If I'd tied it up though, in one of those cool hair fasteners that lots of girls like to wear, he wouldn't have been able to grab hold of it and yank me backward.

All thoughts of hair straighteners and long flowing hair were abruptly wiped from my mind as I was flung around in a full circle. He held tightly to the loose strands and threw me roughly onto the ground.

When I later reflected on the terror of that moment, I clearly recalled watching the scene from above. Isn't that what happens in a near-death experience? That's what I'd read somewhere. I was sure of it. Although at that point, I wasn't even close to death. Right then it was something much more terrifying!

The feeling of floating above and watching the scene beneath unfold is hard to comprehend. Maybe that's what happens in moments of sheer panic?

Why is he covering my mouth? The thought filtered through my subconscious as one rough and calloused hand tried to clamp my mouth closed while the other fumbled clumsily under my skirt. Looking down from overhead, I had an unobstructed view of the desperation in my movements as I shook my head from side to side and fought to break free. But his body weight on top of mine had me pinned to the ground with no means of escape.

It was then that I became aware of a piercing scream. It was a scream that continued on and on and on. Relentlessly, it cut through the night air as the ear-splitting sound emanated with blood-curdling intensity.

I realized then, that he was furiously trying to silence me. Ironically though, the more I swung my head from side to side, trying to free my mouth from his struggling grasp, the louder the sounds became. I really don't think I was aware of it at the time but those screams poured out in an effortless and unstoppable motion from the depths of my throat and I was powerless to stop them.

Looking back, I'm convinced that's what saved me. His frantic attempts to silence me were useless against the adrenaline pumping through my body. Worried the noise would alert attention, he leaped to his feet, raced around the car to the driver's side, jumped in and accelerated at top speed down the road.

Staring in disbelief, I watched the car disappear, the tires screeching loudly and a blast of gravel and dust from the dirt road filling the air. I'd been given a second chance; miraculously my prayers had been answered.

Glancing fearfully around, I attempted to understand what had just happened.

Feeling as though I had witnessed a terrifying movie or a hideous crime scene, I was still in shock but managed to get to my feet and take off in the opposite direction. I had escaped in one piece, alive and breathing; the more I thought about it the more frightening the experience became.

Thick brambles scraped my flesh as I burst through the undergrowth with no idea where I was headed. Blindly, I fled, concerned only with reaching safety. Soon, however, I found myself standing on the side of a busy road, horns honking at me as the cars flew past.

"Hey, want a lift?"

I watched anxiously as a black car slowed to a halt and the window slid down. In full view was an unkempt and disfigured face staring back at me.

Lowering my head, I ignored the taunting voice and kept walking, all the while gripping firmly to the bag that hung from my shoulder. Then, with immense relief, I watched the car speed away, a blast of obscenities pouring from driver through the open window.

Tears streamed down my cheeks. This sort of thing did not happen to me! It was something that I read about in the newspaper or watched on television. How did I, Julia Jones, come to be involved in something so unbelievable and terrifying?

Sobbing quietly, I trudged along the roadside, trying to hide amongst nearby bushes whenever I heard the sound of an oncoming vehicle. I had no idea exactly where I was or how far I had to go. Meanwhile, thoughts of my phone, still sitting on the desk in my room, flashed through my mind.

I had told my mom time and time again that I needed a new phone. It was her old one and was constantly needing to be recharged.

"It just needs a new battery," she reminded me several times over.

But of course, the battery still hadn't been replaced and when I found the phone uncharged before leaving for the party, I decided there was no point in taking it with me.

Up ahead, I saw a blinking neon motel sign flashing brightly. I considered banging on the door in the hope that someone might be able to help me. Though, when I drew closer, I saw the place was in darkness. Hoping for an after-hours bell or some way of alerting the owners, I searched the walls around the unlit door frame. But there was no help in sight.

Just as I was about to give up and keep walking, I noticed a steep driveway leading to an open underground carpark and decided to make my way beyond the parked cars. Anything was better than walking the streets alone so late at night. Heading to a distant corner at the very back, I found a place where I could crouch, hidden by the cars and the blackness of the night.

In my disoriented state, I had no idea of my exact location but when I emerged into the daylight the following morning, I was overcome with relief to discover that I was only a few blocks from home.

Apart from exhaustion, and several scrapes on my arms and legs, I had managed to escape a dangerous situation. But I was sure I'd never forget the trauma and the fear it had caused.

Thankfully, both Mom and Matt were still asleep when I quietly let myself into the house a short time later. Sneaking up the stairs, I carefully side-stepped the squeaky spot that was yet to be repaired by Barry. Endless repairs and renovations. When would all the work finally be completed so I would never have to see his ugly face again? It could not happen too soon.

Those were my last thoughts as I climbed gratefully into bed and laid my head on the pillow. Sleep and rest were all I craved.

Just as I drifted into oblivion, an image of Blake's face floated through my mind, his outstretched hand beckoning me towards him.

Rumors...

I returned to school on Monday, wearing jeans and a long-sleeved shirt to hide the scratches that still covered my skin. I'd decided not to mention the incident to my mother. She'd be furious about my lack of common sense and probably threaten to ground me. Apart from her though, I had no one to talk to. However, when I saw Lisa standing in the hallway waiting for the first bell, she was desperate to hear all the details.

"OMG, Joe is so cute!" she said with a grin. "What happened when he drove you home? Tell me everything!"

Lisa was definitely not someone I'd be happy to share the events of that terrible night with. Along with the other girls, she was nice to me, but not a genuine friend, certainly not one I could trust my secrets with. Since returning to Carindale, I hadn't found anyone who fitted that description. Although, I was hoping that when Millie finally returned from her overseas trip, our close friendship would fall back into place.

Lisa looked at me impatiently. "Come on, Julia. Tell me all! I bet he's a really good kisser!!"

"You've got to be joking! I wouldn't know and I don't want to know!" My abrupt reply was full of loathing; the memory of Friday night, still so clear in my mind.

When I saw her surprised expression, I backed off. She watched me curiously and I could see she was not going to let it go. She thought I was hiding something and was determined to find out what.

A slow grin appeared on her face. "That's not what I heard!"

"What do you mean?" I asked crossly. "What are you talking about?'

"Well, …he told his friend, Jake, who is friends with my sister, Ronnie….that you guys got up to a lot more than just kissing!"

My look of horror stopped Lisa dead in her tracks. Contemplating my reaction, she blurted loudly, "It's okay, Julia. I don't mean to judge you. I'm just telling you what I heard. According to Ronnie, there's a heap of stories going around about what went on after the party."

Noticing the interested glances of the people milling around us, Lisa lowered her voice. "I thought I should let you know. I'm just telling you what Ronnie said."

"Well, Joe is lying, Lisa! Nothing happened. He was drunk and disgusting! And if you must know, I got out of his car and walked home. He's a revolting creep and I hope I never see him again!"

Quietly babbling the words, I desperately hoped she believed me, while at the same time, my stomach filled with dread at the thought of whatever rumors were being spread.

Her expression became skeptical; she wasn't sure if I was telling the truth or not. But it was his word against mine and for the hundredth time, I cursed myself for choosing to accept a ride in the first place.

I was well aware though, that if I mentioned anything more, the whole school would find out and that was the last thing I wanted. Sensing my distress, she decided to change the subject and focused the conversation on herself instead. Even though I had no interest whatsoever in what she was prattling on about, I pretended to show some enthusiasm, while at the same time, a sickly sensation wound through my stomach.

I really was not in the mood to hear about her night with some hot footballer she'd met at the party; certainly not after my own experience. Deep down, I knew I should report what had happened to me, but I couldn't bring myself to do it. That idea seemed as frightening as the incident itself. And besides, it would be his word against mine which was the biggest deterrent of all! I'd heard of similar cases where girls were interrogated by the police and accused of leading the guy on.

As if! I thought to myself, the memory filling me with loathing.

But the real issue lay deeper than that. I was fully aware that in a way, I was the one to blame. Accepting a lift was such a dumb thing to do; especially with someone I hardly knew and who had been drinking all night. It was just plain stupid. So many times over the weekend, I went through the scenario in my mind and finally came to the conclusion that it if I hadn't been so impulsive, the whole incident would have been avoided.

But after hearing what Lisa had said, maybe I made a mistake. Perhaps I should have reported it the very next day. Now it really was his word against my own.

"Make wise choices, Julia!" I could hear my mother's voice, as always, in the back of my head.

It was as clear as a bell and I remembered rolling my eyes at her as I'd mimicked her words sarcastically under my breath. At the time, she'd been harassing me with one of her many lectures, lectures I found so annoying.

Maybe I really should take more advice from my mother! The thought flitted into my subconscious but was quickly shaken away when I remembered her persistent nagging just that morning.

"Julia, have you cleaned your room? As soon as you get home today, I want it cleaned. It's a disgrace! Barry still has to repair your wardrobe door and I'm embarrassed to let him even enter your room at the moment!"

The mere mention of his name had been enough to set me off and I immediately began a screaming match with her, yelling at her to come to her senses about her sleazy friend, who called himself a tradesman. That provoked the reaction I'd been looking for and with a satisfied smirk, I threw my dishes into the sink full of water, splashing soap suds and water all over the benchtop, the kitchen window, and the floor. I then stormed out of the house ensuring I slammed the front door with the loudest bang that I could possibly muster.

The truth of the matter was that I simply could not stand to be around her anymore. She constantly irritated me and I decided to ask my friends if anyone wanted to hang out at the mall later that afternoon. Anything was better than going home to face my mom!

Thankfully, the bell for first period sounded and the image of my mother's angry face faded away as everyone made their way to class.

English was my first lesson of the day. It was a class I had always looked forward to, primarily because of our teacher, Miss Fitzroy. Unfortunately, though, the week before she was unexpectedly transferred to another school.

Everyone considered her the coolest teacher ever and did not want her to leave. As well as being really young and very pretty, she always dressed in the most fashionable clothes. The girls constantly commented on her outfits and we had so much fun chatting with her after class about fashion and the latest styles that she wore.

Most importantly, the way she taught English made it really enjoyable, which was such a refreshing change from the boring lessons we'd all experienced in the past. It was ridiculously unfair that she had to leave.

As soon as I saw our new teacher, who we soon learned was named Miss Bromley, it was instantly obvious that she was different in every way imaginable to our beloved Miss Fitz.

In place of the beautiful young woman who had laughed with us and made English class a fun place to be, was a short, dumpy middle-aged lady with a screechy voice who quickly told everyone to take a seat as soon as they entered the room.

"Hurry up, people. Time is very valuable and you're wasting it!"

What an introduction! I sat down and looked curiously in her direction.

We were asked to open our books and begin the exercises on page 104. The next instruction was to complete the ten pages that followed or those pages would be added to our homework for the night.

"Is she serious?" I could hear the disbelief in the male voice behind me.

When I glanced around, the same disbelieving expression was on the face of every student in the room.

"Yes, I am deadly serious!" she replied sharply and frowned at the boy who had spoken. "Any more comments and I'll add an extra ten pages to *your* homework for tonight."

Her response was enough to immediately silence the class and as I looked around once more, I saw that no one was prepared to argue. I think it was the quietest I had ever seen the group, and hardly a word was said during the entire double period. Finally, the bell sounded for morning recess and we were given permission to leave.

As soon as we were out of earshot of our new English teacher, everyone's opinions could be heard.

"That totally sucks!"

"I can't believe SHE replaced Miss Fitz!"

"OMG! One lesson and already I can't stand her!"

It was so unfair to be stuck with her as our new teacher and I agreed wholeheartedly with the complaints coming from the others.

Just as I joined my friends in our usual spot for morning break, I spotted Sara, walking past and deep in conversation with the girl at her side. Quickly, I looked away, hoping that she wouldn't notice me. It was the first time I'd seen her since the incident with the voodoo doll in my locker; a memory I preferred to put behind me.

Unable to help myself, I stole a fleeting glimpse in her direction and as luck would have it, she happened to gaze my way at that very moment. My heart sank when, with her eyes focused on me, I saw her open her mouth to speak. Instead, though, she chose to give me a spiteful glare. Probably hoping to provoke a reaction, she continued to stare as she strolled past. It was a look that made my stomach turn and the air between us was thick with tension.

My pulse quickened with anxiety at the evil look she was directing toward me. The vivid blue of her eyes was the color that haunted my dreams.

"What's her problem?" Beth asked quietly after Sara had finally moved away.

"Yeah! Did you see the look she gave you, Julia? What was that all about?" Lisa's remark added to the sinking dismay that was creeping down my spine.

"I have no idea!" I lied, desperately wishing I was any place but there, with Sara in my midst.

I quickly changed the subject, while trying to rid myself of the uncomfortable sensation that continued to wind through me.

Unexpected...

My shopping expedition after school proved to be more than I had bargained for. Although I could have just gone on my own, I knew it would be much more fun to hang out with one of the girls from school.

As it turned out, Lisa was the only one available that afternoon and when I suggested the idea to her, she eagerly agreed. "I have a heap of homework to do, but who cares!"

It was evident from her keen response that she didn't have to be persuaded and I was glad to have an excuse to avoid going straight home, myself.

On the bus, heading towards the shopping mall, she told me of a brand new store that had recently opened and which stocked some really cool designer clothes.

"We should go and check it out. You never know, they may have a sale on," she said hopefully. "The clothes are gorgeous but it's super expensive!"

Her words showed her frustration. I had originally thought Lisa received a fairly generous weekly allowance which would explain all the lovely clothes she already owned. Though I guessed that may not actually be the case.

She was still determined we should have a browse and with a little prompting on her part, we were soon in the change rooms, trying on a variety of really pretty tops, designer jeans, and jackets and as well, some colorful knit sweaters. I quickly fell in love with the long sleeved shirt that she'd picked out for me and had convinced me to try on. It was black and fitted, with a cool design printed on the front. I knew it would match perfectly with my new skirt but when I looked at the price tag, I could see it was way beyond what I could afford to pay.

Lisa looked at me thoughtfully but then continued trying on the various items that she had hanging in her cubicle. Eventually, she settled on a pair of gorgeous white high-waist skinny jeans that looked amazing on her. She had such a beautiful figure and the jeans accentuated her shape.

Looking on with envy, I agreed that she definitely had to buy them. That happened to be all the encouragement she needed and with barely any hesitation whatsoever, she pulled out her savings card and took the jeans to the cash register. Chatting in a friendly manner with the sales assistant, she smiled politely and keyed in her pin number. All the while, I stood watching and trying to come to terms with the fact that she had just spent $200 on a pair of jeans without even flinching, even after complaining earlier that the clothes were too expensive.

After exiting the store, we decided to indulge in a hot chocolate at our favorite café. Sitting in a booth towards the back, I looked on astonished, as she opened my backpack and discreetly pulled a pile of brand new clothes with tickets still attached, into view on the seat between us.

Grinning delightedly at my reaction, she explained. "Julia, it's so easy! All you have to do is distract the assistant with a sale and then walk out. Because you've bought something, they would never suspect that you've taken other things from the rack. It works every time!"

Astonished, I stared at her, overcome with disbelief, "What! You stole these things?"

Horrified, and realizing the full extent of what she had done, I blurted angrily, "But you put those things in *my* bag, Lisa!

You know there are security cameras everywhere! What if I was caught?"

I glared incredulously at the items she had shoved deep inside my backpack. In total, the pile of clothes was easily worth at least $500 and I'd had no idea they were hidden in my bag. I pictured the two of us in the store and could not understand how she had managed to stash them away without my knowledge. Dumbfounded, I stared silently at the clothes as I visualized myself walking out, my bag crammed with stolen goods. Trembling fearfully, I considered the consequences if my bag had been checked.

"I can't keep these, Lisa! We have to take them back!"

It was her turn to stare at me disbelievingly. "Are you kidding? No way, Julia! I just went to all that trouble and spent $200 on a pair of jeans, just to get all this stuff. There's no way, I'm taking them back!"

I shook my head as the waitress placed our cups of hot chocolate on the table in front of us, while Lisa subtly shoved the clothes out of sight beneath the table top.

"And besides," she continued, "how are we supposed to return them without getting caught? That's the most ridiculous thing I've ever heard!"

Nausea rose in my throat as I remembered the last time I had attempted to steal from a clothing store. A security guard had caught me and chased me down the street. I was terrified that the police would turn up on my doorstep and imagined the shocked reaction from my parents. I felt so guilty afterward, I decided to take the item back to the store and hand it to the sales assistant, who was speechless as she stood listening to my apology. She then congratulated me on making the right choice and acknowledged that it would have taken quite a lot of courage to do so. I didn't deserve the praise though. I knew it then and I still know it now.

"You're no fun, Julia!" Lisa whined. "The clothes in that store are so expensive. How else can we afford clothes this quality? These are designer labels you know! The other girls are going to be so jealous when they see us wearing them. And besides, this black top looks fantastic on you!"

I stared thoughtfully at the silky black top that I had tried on and fallen in love with. I knew that it fitted me perfectly. In the past, I had admired that particular label and dreamed of owning something so stylish. The temptation to keep it was gradually becoming too much to resist.

"I don't know!" I responded. "I think I'll feel too guilty every time I wear it!"

"I tell you what," she replied, in her usual persuasive manner, "take it home and have a think about it. If you decide you want to keep it, then great! But if not, you can just give it to me. It's a gorgeous top. If you don't want it, I'll have it for myself!"

With a deep sigh, I reluctantly agreed; although, I had to admit that I was definitely keen to keep the top. It may be the only chance I ever had to own clothing so special, especially while I was still at school and on such a limited allowance.

Sitting thoughtfully next to her, I pictured the look on Blake's face, and Lisa's words sounded in my mind once more. "The guys won't be able to resist you in that top, Julia!"

A small but guilty smile began to form on my lips as I imagined Blake's reaction. I wasn't interested in anyone else; he was the only one I wanted to impress.

Shock...

I burst through the front door late that afternoon, planning to race up to my room with the stolen item intact in my school bag. I was ready to hide the designer top in the depths of my cupboard after insisting that Lisa take the rest of the clothes home with her. As it were, I was struggling with the thought of a stolen $120 top in my possession. There was no way I could ever agree to take any additional items as well.

At that point, I was still unsure if I should keep the top or not. On the bus ride home, I pictured myself sneaking it back into the clothing store. But I knew I didn't have the courage for that. When I faced a similar scenario back in middle school, it had taken huge resolve to own up to the sales assistant who greeted me at the store entrance.

I was a different person back then; an A-grade student full of promise, or so my mother kept telling me. Her support and belief in me no longer existed though. I was on my own with no one to share my deepest secrets with.

It had been a long time since I opened up to my mom. The thought of doing that now was beyond comprehension. She was no longer a person I wanted to talk to, certainly not about anything private.

She was betraying her family for the sake of a slimy tradesman and I found that so gut-wrenching, it made me sick to my stomach. It was difficult to even think of her as my mother anymore and I had to fight the urge to scream in frustration whenever she was in sight.

Already uneasy about the stolen top, when I entered the house and found myself face to face with Barry, I was instantly overwhelmed. Clinging tightly to my school bag, I barely dared to acknowledge him. Without uttering a word, he stared at me, his gaze so intense, I felt more uncomfortable than ever. I cringed as I huddled closer to the wall, trying to stand as far away from him as possible as he walked past. It was an involuntary action that I had no control over.

I'd promised myself I would stand up to him though. I had already decided that was the only way to deal with him and I summoned the strength I needed.

His gaze lingered as he waited for my reaction. His intention was clearly to upset me. He was aware of the effect he had and enjoyed every second of watching me squirm. He was such a jerk, a sleazy, disgusting jerk and I wanted to get as far away from him as possible.

Taking a deep breath, I lifted my chin defiantly and scowled with loathing. I couldn't let him get to me. If I did, he'd win. It was all a game to him, I could see that now, and I couldn't give him that power over me.

He grinned creepily as he walked past, his eyes burning into mine before heading up the stairs to the bathroom. I held my head high and stared back, determined to appear strong. But it was the sideways glance and evil grin that made me cringe once more. I'd always thought he was a creep but at that moment, I knew for sure I was right.

What on earth did my mother see in him? It was totally beyond me and something I struggled to understand. But no matter how much I tried, she never believed my stories of how uncomfortable he made me feel.

"Oh, Julia, you're being so silly!" she had exclaimed, a few days earlier. "Barry is such a lovely man. He's just being friendly, that's all!"

Deep down, I knew she was enjoying his attention. Her whole demeanor changed when he was in the house and I was convinced she was making excuses for him to return. But surely by now, he had finished all the odd jobs, as she kept calling them.

I caught a glimpse of my dad's smiling face, standing alongside Mom in the photo frame hanging on the wall. It was a collage that I had put together for their last wedding anniversary and was filled with photos of the four of us, Mom, Dad, Matt and I, happy, smiling, family photos. They were the type you'd expect to see in a collection such as that one, hanging in full view on the wall that led up the stairway.

Later that evening after Barry had finally left, I gazed longingly at that image. I was headed to the living room for a 'family conference' when it caught my eye.

I grimaced when I heard Mom use that expression. *Family conference. What a joke!* I couldn't remember the last time we'd had a family meeting, as she usually liked to refer to them, but they were always held when Dad was in the house and we were a proper family, with all family members present.

"Sit down," she said quietly when Matt finally poked his head around the door. "There's something I need to tell you!"

She was having trouble making eye contact with either of us and was acting strangely. Her awkward manner was combined with a hesitant frown and I was certain that whatever she had to say was not going to be good news. I could feel it. The sinking feeling in my stomach was too real, too powerful to ignore. And then fear took over as I took in her words, too stunned to speak.

"What are you saying, Mom?" Matt's incredulous expression filled me with sadness.

He had no idea of what had been going on around him. Wrapped up like a cocoon in his own little world that consisted of senior high school, his friends, girls and computer games, he'd been completely oblivious. But at least she'd had the decency to ask Barry to leave before breaking the news to us.

My intuition had been right once again and although I was shocked to the core, I had to admit that I saw it coming. All the signs had been there.

"I'm moving into the city with Barry, into his apartment. We're going to live together."

While Matt stared at her in confusion, I was wrought with anger, a sensation so intense, I'd never felt that worked up before.

And then I lashed out. "So, you're just going to leave us? Walk out on Dad and Matt and I…just like that?" Shaking my head in disbelief, I glared at her in disgust.

"I don't get it!" Matt's pitiful voice cut through the silence as he looked from her to me and back to her again.

"She's leaving us, Matt. She's moving in with that creep; that sleazy carpenter who's been spending so much time in our house since Dad left. She's probably even been sleeping with him in Dad's bed!"

She stared at me speechless, the guilt written clearly on her face.

"I HATE YOU!!!!!!!!!!!" Spitting the words at her, I raced up the stairs to my room and slammed the door closed.

I had to get away. I could not stand being in her presence for a single moment longer.

How could she do this to us?

How could she do it to Dad?

My head spun with emotion and a whirlwind of questions.

How would Dad react when he heard?

Did he know already?

Had she told him yet?

And what about Matt and I; we were still at school! Had she even considered that small detail?

I paced around my room, unable to stand still, unable to sit. I was overwhelmed beyond despair. Catching sight of the silky black fabric that was poking out of the top of my opened school bag, I pulled it free, scrunched it into a ball and threw it in the wastepaper basket.

I didn't care about designer clothes. I didn't care at all. I just wanted my family back. I wanted things back to the way they were! We were so happy living in the country. Life there was easy. I had my friends, I had my beautiful pony, Bella and I had my family.

How could everything have gone so wrong?

Distractions....

The weeks passed by and each day blended into the next. Matt and I grew accustomed to having the house to ourselves and my mother's visits became more and more infrequent.

To begin with, she came home every weekend, to buy food and cook and clean, to do all the things that a mother usually does; everything except connecting with her children.

I barely talked to her when she was in the house and usually tried to find excuses to go out. Otherwise, I just hid in my room. Matt rarely spoke about our situation at all. Although he seemed to be okay, I suspected he was hurting even more than me.

Unable to comprehend how our mother could desert us, I struggled to understand how a mother was able to walk out on her children. I knew that we weren't classified as kids anymore. Matt was in his final year at school and both of us were capable of looking after ourselves, but it just wasn't the norm. How could she even consider leaving Dad and breaking up our family? What sort of mother does that kind of thing?

Regardless though, Matt and I were surviving, the way Mom said we would. According to her, she had no doubt whatsoever that we'd be okay.

"I wouldn't leave if I didn't think you'd cope, Julia. Ever since you were a little girl, I could always rely on you. You've always been so mature and grown up. And besides, I'll be home every weekend to check up on you both."

Then she packed her bags and left. But if she thought that a phone call every evening was enough to make things right, she was wrong! For me anyway. I wasn't interested in talking to her. I always had very little to say and preferred to pass the phone over to Matt who would only give her one-word responses. I was pleased about that. She didn't deserve anything more.

She soon stopped ringing quite so often. Her nightly phone calls quickly dwindled to once every few days and then maybe once a week. She started visiting less and less. But that suited me perfectly.

When I tried to analyze it all, I came to the conclusion that the main reason I was coping so well, was because I'd pushed it all to the back of my mind. If she didn't want to be with us, then good riddance! I didn't want her around anyway!

At least I didn't have to put up with her constant nagging any longer.

"Clean your room, Julia!"

"Do your homework, Julia!"

"Get off the phone, Julia!"

"Shuttttt – uppppppp!!!!!" I could hear myself screaming those words at the sound of her irritating voice and was glad to be rid of her.

There was something that did bother me though. Nearly a month later, I could still picture the image on my dad's face when he returned home. It was the day after she'd moved out and it's an image I'll never forget. I was so sad, so sorry for him. The sorrow and loss that filled his features as he walked into our family home and discovered that, no it wasn't a joke, nor was it a made up story or some crazy dream that he had abruptly awoken from. She really had left.

It was too sad for words.

When I found him later that night sitting alone in his favorite kitchen chair, I was able to connect with his sadness and my heart went out to him.

I'd never seen my father cry before. When the tears poured down his cheeks, tears of my own began to fall. As I held him tightly, we both sobbed; choking tears that neither of us could hold back. Sitting on his lap just like I used to as a little girl, we clung to each other and could not let go. It was the saddest moment of my life.

With the passing of time, my circumstances eventually became routine. Matt and I lived in our family home mostly on our own and I quickly grew accustomed to that.

Dad's roster changed once again and he was unable to come home every weekend. Sometimes he returned once a fortnight. But we managed to adjust remarkably well. He transferred money into my bank account each week and I took turns with my brother to buy the groceries. Although, I was usually the one to do the food shopping. If I were to leave it to Matt, we would probably starve.

It was pretty fortunate that I was a reasonable cook. I don't think Matt could live on two-minute noodles for very long, and I enjoyed experimenting with different recipes each night.

While my school work began to suffer and my grades dropped, I didn't really care. I had more important things to focus on.

That included Ky Samford, a really cool and very good looking guy in my science class. He sat at the back of the room which was probably why I hadn't noticed him before. With longish brown hair that he constantly flicked off his brow, he was so cute and I couldn't stop thinking about him.

When I sat down to do some homework one evening, the first I'd attempted all week, I barely managed to complete the task because I spent the first hour or so scribbling his name on my notepad. I hadn't yet mentioned him to anyone and I was pretty sure they hadn't noticed his discreet glances in my direction either.

Except for Blake that was! I caught him staring at me in our last lesson of the day but at the same time, so was Ky.

Blake hadn't come near me for ages, although I felt him watching me from time to time. I did try talking to him but he simply mumbled a few words and made excuses to move away. If he refused to talk to me then why was he bothering to take notice of me? It didn't make sense.

Lately, I'd noticed him hanging out with a really pretty girl in our grade. I wasn't sure what was going on between them but they appeared to be very friendly. At one point, I even spotted him brushing hair out of her eyes.

Meanwhile, I was happy to have Ky as a distraction, one I badly needed to help take my mind off Blake and all the other dramas going on in my life.

I'd tried to keep my parents' separation a secret from my friends. I also asked Matt not to tell anyone at school but he said they'd find out anyway, so we may as well be the ones to share the news.

Great! Want to hear some gossip, guys? You don't need the soap operas on television; my home life is much more interesting than any of those shows you're all so hooked on!

At first, I thought it'd be really embarrassing for everyone to know that my parents had split up; especially the circumstances! I mean…who wants their mother's affair to become public knowledge at school?

I was horrified at the thought of people finding out and could easily imagine their reactions. But in the end, I decided to take my brother's advice. Reluctantly, I shared the latest gossip, the latest news. And of course, out of everyone, Lisa was the one who probed for all the details. She was fascinated. But all in all, everyone was genuinely sympathetic and they still keep asking after me to check if I'm okay. I've really appreciated that. It means a lot to know that they do genuinely care.

Naturally, somewhere along the grapevine, Sara also found out. And she made sure I was fully aware that she knew.

"Oh, my gosh, Julia, I heard about your parents!" She approached me from behind but I would recognize her voice anywhere. "Is it true that your mother has moved out with some guy she was having an affair with?" The fake sympathy dripping from her tone irritated me more than anything.

When she continued on, the sarcasm was thick in her voice. "Poor Julia! Are you okay, sweetie? Let me know if there's anything I can do to help."

I couldn't believe her condescending manner. She really was unbelievable! I was fuming inside and it took all my self-control not to lash out at her. Right then, I hated her more than ever!

Though, I reminded myself to be grateful because I hadn't seen her around at all lately. Perhaps she'd finally managed to get over her need for revenge or whatever it was she was trying to inflict on me. However, I had a sneaking suspicion that she would always hold a grudge and I reminded myself to stay alert.

Long blond hair flowed in waves down the length of her back as she strutted past. Her persona of confidence and self-obsession was on display for everyone to see and I was consumed with loathing.

But there was something different about her. At first, I couldn't place it, then after a few moments, I knew.

She was wearing a familiar red skirt, one that I also owned and that I had seen her wear on other occasions. But instead of being fitted to her slim figure, it hung loosely around her hips and thighs, so much so that she needed a belt to hold it in place.

Her skirts were always tightly fitted, which was why this detail stood out. In fact, I didn't recall ever seeing her wear a loose style before.

I wondered if she'd been dieting, something totally unnecessary as she had a perfect body and there was no need for her to lose weight. I was curious as to the cause but then figured she'd probably been ill which would explain her recent absence from school.

As she continued along the walkway and disappeared from sight, I spotted Ky making his way through the parking lot and all thoughts of Sara disappeared from my mind.

I'd heard he was older than most of the kids in my grade

and already had his drivers' license as well as his own car. It was the coolest thing ever! When the bus pulled up, I quickly boarded and hurried down the aisle looking for an empty window seat so I could watch him reverse out from his parking space and drive away.

I wonder where he lives? The thought crossed my mind as the bus drove onto the main road. *I'll have to find an excuse to talk to him!*

As I sat picturing his smiling face, trying to plot ways to coincidentally grasp his attention, I had no idea that the opportunity would arise in the least expected manner and much sooner than I ever anticipated.

Surprises...

Later that evening, I started my laptop, aiming to finish the English homework that Miss Bromley had set for us. Unlike the homework that was given for other subjects, no one dared to show up at school without their English completed.

Within seconds of my computer screen lighting up, I went straight to Facebook, unable to resist the temptation. Since my mother walked out, I pretty much had a free reign and no longer needed to sneak around behind her back. This unfamiliar freedom allowed me to have open access to all the social media sites, just like most normal teenagers around the world. And in no time whatsoever, I'd become addicted.

After learning how to block unwanted people from my account, I was safe in the knowledge that my mother couldn't stalk my page and find out what I was up to. Not that I really cared what she thought, but it was my private place and I didn't want her knowing my business. As well, I'd heard stories from friends about the embarrassing comments and posts their parents were constantly adding to their pages and that was something I wanted to avoid at all costs. Luckily for me, my dad's computer skills were almost non-existent, and Facebook was totally foreign to him so I had no concerns there.

Over the past week, I had searched for Millie. In the beginning, I had no success at all and because none of the girls I hung out with at school were friends with her on FB, they couldn't help me to locate her. I'd begun to suspect that she may not even have a Facebook account anymore.

Then that morning, by a stroke of luck, I happened to stumble across her page. In typical Millie style, she had listed herself using her first and middle names and when her profile picture popped up, I instantly recognized the image of the friend I had never managed to replace.

I added her as a friend and typed a super long message, trying to apologize for not staying in contact. We hadn't spoken for so long and I felt guilty about being so slack. Deciding I was over-thinking things, I pressed send and hoped for a reply.

When I saw her response, it jumped out at me through the computer screen and I could easily hear the excitement in her voice as I quickly scanned her words.

"JULIAAAAAAAAAAA!!!!!! OMG!!!!! I AM SOOOOOOO EXCITED!!!!

I CAN'T BELIEVE YOU'RE BACK IN CARINDALE!!

I'VE MISSED YOU SOOOOOOOOOO MUCH!!!!"

The upper case letters caused an ecstatic smile to form on my face. Immediately overcome with emotion, I began to laugh and cry at the same time.

Realizing that she was online right at that moment, I quickly replied and our messages flowed effortlessly back and forth. Though I was so happy to hear from her that I could barely type.

Pausing for her next reply, I glanced nostalgically at the photo frame that still sat on my bookshelf, the one with Millie and I, arms wrapped around each other, looking the happiest we had ever been. The wonderful memories of our middle school days together came pouring back and I was hit with excited anticipation at the thought of her return.

Before signing off, she reminded me that she would arrive home in three weeks' time. It was so soon and I could hardly wait for that day to come.

After reading her responses through once again, I was convinced that everything would be okay between us. She was clearly as excited as me at the prospect of seeing one another again and I was both relieved and overjoyed at the same time.

Unable to focus on school work, especially boring English homework, I ignored the books that lay spread across my desk and started looking through Millie's personal page. There were so many wonderful photos that she had uploaded whilst on her trip and it certainly looked like her family had been having an amazing vacation.

When I came across a fabulous family pic with each of them standing side by side, their smiles an obvious indication of how happy they all were, I felt a twinge of envy. My family had once been that happy and we had often discussed the idea of family trips abroad. But there was never enough money for luxuries such as those and now it appeared that we wouldn't have the opportunity again.

Holding back the tears that threatened at the corners of my eyes, I glanced at the books lying haphazardly on my desk. Just as I reached across to log out of FB, I noticed a new friend request and wondered who the person might be.

As I'd previously had a couple of random requests from guys I didn't know, I had become very cautious. Especially after checking their pages and discovering they were friends of Joe, the creep who I foolishly accepted a ride home with after the party a few weeks earlier. But why were they suddenly interested in me?

I had already put the terrifying incident behind me, locked it in a hidden compartment of my memory banks. Confronted with the memory once again, Lisa's warning about rumors spreading soon after the party had ended came rushing back.

Hopefully, the friend requests had nothing to do with rumors Joe's friends may have heard. Wanting to avoid all contact with any of them, Joe included, I immediately deleted their requests. But now a new one stared back at me.

Tentatively, I placed my fingers over the keyboard and clicked the icon to find out who it had come from.

The gasp that followed was one of surprise or possibly even shock. I wasn't sure how to describe my reaction, but the name that stared back was so unexpected!

Confusion...

My computer screen displayed his profile picture. Next to that was the Confirm or Delete Request link.

"OMG! I can't believe this!" The words escaped my lips and I jumped back in my seat, my fingers hovering over the keyboard.

"OMG!" I breathed again, sheer disbelief working its way through my senses along with a nervous excitement.

"This is freaky! Do I accept or not?" I spoke the words aloud, even though there was no one else in the room.

As I stared at the profile pic, I heard an insistent voice inside my head. "Yes, of course, you should accept! You stupid girl, why wouldn't you??!!"

I clicked the button and waited. I have no idea why I waited but I was frozen in place. It was as though I had done something forbidden; something risky that was going to lead to all kinds of trouble, although I had no idea why or what.

Ky Samford had a bad boy image. It was the kind that almost took my breath away, and my instincts told me that he was different to most of the guys at school.

Just that afternoon, as I was leaving the school grounds, he had turned and looked at me. It was quite strange the way it happened, almost as if a silent voice had called his name and for one brief second, our eyes had met. The moment was fleeting but I had definitely sensed some sort of connection. At the time, I thought I'd imagined it but that would not explain the abrupt spark which filled my senses and the flutter of butterflies in the depths of my stomach.

I had no idea why I'd never noticed him before. Although I guess I was wrapped up in thoughts of Blake, and in all my problems at home. I was so deeply entrenched in my own little shell of misery that I hadn't even realized Ky existed.

Now that I was aware of him, he was all I could think about. And right then, he was the reason I was ignoring my homework.

Before long, I heard the sound I'd been hoping for. That little blip noise, the one that alerts you to a new message.

Hi

One single word, one single syllable, but it said so much more.

Nervously, I replied. *Hi*

My stomach was doing somersaults as I sat there, tense and excited. And then, that wonderful blip noise sounded again. A wide smile spread across my face as I read the next message.

You have nice eyes

"OMG!" I yelled aloud and laughed.

I couldn't believe he had said that. I re-read his words... *You have nice eyes.*

No one I knew spoke that way, certainly not any of the boys at my new school, Blake included.

I could just imagine my friends, Lisa in particular, scoffing, "He's weird!" I heard her voice clearly inside my head.

He was not her type; I knew that with certainty. He was too

aloof, too reserved and unusual to appeal to Lisa. She liked the buff football types, the ones who had muscles bulging on muscles. They were the ones that she constantly drooled over. But there was something very different about Ky, something that appealed to me. A mad fluttering of butterflies, as well as a tingling of excitement, caused goose bumps to form on my skin. It was the same sensation I'd always felt with Blake in the past, whenever I was near him, whenever I looked into his eyes. Guiltily, I recalled the instant pleasure that was created by the mere touch of his hand on my arm.

But he and I were over now. And after breaking up with Sara he had moved onto someone else. At least that appeared to be the case. I thought fleetingly of Monica, the pretty girl at school who he'd been spending so much time with lately. I was hit with a strong pang of jealousy as an image of the two of them, so familiar in each other's company, flashed through my mind.

Filled with resentment, I stared at the computer screen once again.

Without giving it another moment's thought, I entered one word before logging off.

Thanks!

That was all I could think of to say and I didn't dare wait for a response. It was all too much and my stomach churned with the anxiety of the moment. Then I remembered something that put me completely out of sorts. Science, the one class that Ky and I shared, happened to be scheduled for first period the following morning. Nervously, I contemplated the thought of seeing him when I entered the room.

Maybe I was making something out of nothing though.

Perhaps he was just being friendly and I was imagining a romance that was never going to happen.

Or was I was simply hoping for a replacement for the love of my life, the one whose presence at school continued to haunt me? Could I really just be searching for a distraction to take the place of Blake? The only boy I had ever truly loved.

If that were the case, why did Ky have such an intense effect on me? I barely knew him. I had never even spoken to him in person.

With a frustrated sigh, I glanced at my desk and stared at the English assignment that beckoned me. With so many thoughts and distractions swirling around inside my head, I struggled to focus.

That was until I thought of Miss Bromley's screeching voice and the promise of her detention class for any students with incomplete homework. This proved to be the motivation I needed.

Taking a deep breath, I picked up a pen and started writing.

Concerned...

On edge, I entered the science lab. None of my close friends shared the class with me and I usually sat at any random seat near the front. That morning though, I decided to head towards the back of the room. Without glancing around, I found an unoccupied seat in the second last row, opened my bag and pulled out my science book.

Ky wasn't in any of the seats within view, so if he was in the room, he had to be at the very back. With my head down, I completed the tasks in the text as instructed by our teacher while desperately trying to resist the temptation to look behind me.

My stomach was a mess of nerves as I scribbled notes from the board onto the blank page of my notebook. Eventually, I decided to risk a quick glance. When I turned my head, I spotted him, sitting in the rear corner and instantly, he looked up and stared my way.

"OMG! OMG!" I breathed the words under my breath as I whipped back around towards the front of the room.

I couldn't believe that he'd caught me staring. That was so embarrassing!

My stomach felt queasy as I attempted, with little success, to focus on the teacher's voice. Then, without warning, I heard my name being called.

"Would you like to answer that question for us, Julia?" Mr. Blandford's booming voice could be heard above all else and my face turned a flaming red.

My blank expression clearly displayed the fact that I had no idea what he was talking about and my entire body heated up. Frowning with disapproval, he scanned the class in the hope that another student may have the answer he was looking for. He then asked a girl by the name of Grace who was sitting directly behind me. She knew the answers to just about everything and I grimaced at her quick response. It was full of detail and included all the correct technical terms as well.

No wonder she was top of the class. For our last exam, she submitted an essay that was such a high standard, Mr. Blandford was still raving about it. Her academic ability was incredible and I envied her high results.

Lisa, Beth and the others always said she must spend every waking minute studying or doing homework, which they considered a huge waste of valuable time. Secretly though, I admired her efforts and wished I could have better study habits, myself.

Grateful that all the attention was directed away from me, I turned to Grace and listened to another of her flawless anecdotes. Often what she said was beyond the comprehension of most of the class. Sometimes I wondered if she may even be smarter than our teacher.

As I attempted to understand what she was talking about, I had a burning need to glance in Ky's direction. Unable to fight the impulse, I pretended to focus on Grace, while my eyes flicked to the rear corner.

I locked eyes with him and his mouth curved into a small grin. His dark eyes were intense as they stared directly into mine. Gulping, I whipped back around to the front and tried to control the wild sensation of butterflies dancing crazily inside me.

When the lesson ended and everyone stood up to leave, I gathered my books and joined the throng heading for the door, not daring to glance back.

Reaching the hallway, I saw Lisa exiting her class. To my dismay, she grabbed my arm and led me along the corridor.

She'd been invited on a date by some hot guy from another school and was desperate to share her news. She hadn't yet mentioned his name, not that I was particularly interested. All I wanted was to make eye contact with Ky and I searched for him amongst the milling students in the hallway. I glanced around the crowd, but there was no sign of him anywhere.

Disappointed, I followed Lisa into the room and sat down next to her. Rather than focusing on the lesson though, I found myself engrossed in thoughts of Ky and the beautiful features that adorned his handsome face.

When the bell finally sounded for morning recess, I rushed to the door where I scanned the crowd once more, but there was still no sign of the one person I had hoped to see.

Lisa, oblivious to what was going on inside my head, continued talking about her upcoming date for the weekend, keen to share all the details. Noticing a sudden change in her tone, I looked at her curiously.

"Julia, I need to tell you something." Her eyes darted nervously in all directions and for some reason, she seemed uncomfortable.

"You know how I went to a party on the weekend? Well, I ended up hanging out with some really cool people. Actually, one of them was a guy you've met before."

Alarm bells rang in my head and I tuned in carefully to what she was saying. Who could she be referring to and why was she so nervous?

"You know Joe? The guy who drove you home from that party we went to last month? Well, he was there on Saturday night; he turned up with a few of his friends."

I stared at her uneasily as her words filtered through to my brain.

"Anyway, I know you said you weren't interested in him, but I think he's really hot. And we kind of hooked up at the party. Now he's asked me out on a date. We're going to the movies this weekend."

The words tumbled from her mouth as my expression filled with disbelief.

"What?" she asked defensively. "Why are you looking at me like that? You said you didn't like him, so what's the problem?"

"Lisa, he's a creep! You can do so much better than him!" Her revelation had me frozen to the spot.

"I knew you'd be like this, Julia, I just knew it! You're jealous because he wants to take me out and he's not interested in you!"

I shook my head, desperately wanting her to understand but not sure how I could explain. "That's not true, Lisa. He's the biggest creep I've ever met; you really should stay away from him!"

"He told me you'd say that!" she snapped angrily. "He told me you were all over him that night, but he just wasn't interested! All he offered to do was take you home, but you wanted more!"

My jaw dropped and I stood there speechless. I had no idea what to say. I wanted to warn her but it was obvious she was not going to listen. Joe had her convinced and she would never believe me, I was certain of it.

"Yeah, whatever!" Her sharp retort was followed by an irritated shake of her head as she headed off on her own, down the hallway.

With a sickening sensation working its way through me, I watched her flick her long, blond hair out of her eyes as she hurried to catch up to the other girls. Instinctively, I knew our relationship would never be the same, not while she was dating that creep. My head spun as her words registered in my mind. He'd convinced her to believe he was some type of nice guy. As well as that, he had told her lies about me in order to cover up the terrible way he behaved. He had literally attacked me and was trying to hide that fact.

Apart from the rumors he was spreading, I was genuinely concerned for Lisa's safety. I couldn't believe that of all people, she would accept a date from Joe. I knew what he was capable of and the mere thought of him caused nausea to rise in my throat.

Rushing to the bathroom, I splashed cold water over my face and then stared at my reflection in the mirror. I had been so stupid to accept a ride home with him that night. The scene that I wanted to erase from my mind haunted me once more. Lisa had no idea what she was in for and I wondered if I could persuade her otherwise. If anything happened, I would never forgive myself.

Lisa was a huge flirt and loved any attention that guys gave her. Regardless of that, I knew all she wanted was a boyfriend; a genuine relationship with a boy who she could depend on and who cared about her. But Joe was not the one. At the very least, he would use her and hurt her. There was no doubt in my mind.

When I entered my next class, I dodged the spare seat next to Lisa, who had put her bag on the desk and made it quite clear that I wasn't welcome to sit there. Finding a spot by myself next to a window, the drone of the teacher's voice became a background hum.

Three weeks until Millie returned; that is what she had said. I thought of our online chat the night before and how easy it had been to connect with her again.

At that moment, I missed her more than anything and all I could do was hope that the next three weeks passed by as quickly as possible.

A Favorite Pastime...

After stopping at the supermarket on the way home from school, I dumped the groceries on the kitchen bench and put the cold food in the refrigerator. As I packed the items away, I reflected on the fact that Lisa had most likely discarded me as a friend. Each time I ventured near her during the afternoon, she avoided eye contact and finally, I gave up trying to talk to her. By accepting Joe's story over mine, she'd have to learn the hard way and if she wasn't willing to listen to me, there was nothing I could do.

Hopefully, though, the other girls wouldn't be influenced by her sudden change in attitude towards me. Otherwise, I'd be forced to find a different group to hang out with, at least until Millie returned. Once again, I counted the days until her arrival.

As I continued to pack away the food, I considered the situation for my brother and I. Most of the time, it was just the two of us living in the house alone. Although this had become normal for us, my friends struggled to accept the idea. I had tried to explain on several occasions that my dad came home as often as he could and as well as that, Matt was eighteen years of age, so he was considered an adult and a legal guardian.

"He doesn't act like an adult," I laughed, "but we're used to being on our own now and it's really no big deal."

Even though Matt was legally old enough to be in charge, I'd become the mom of the household. In the course of events, it was something that had occurred naturally and through no planning on my part.

Often, I heard myself nagging him to clean up his mess and hang up his wet towels after using the shower. I also regularly harassed him to do his laundry.

"Seriously, Matt, how hard can it be? All you have to do is open the lid of the washing machine, pour in some detergent and push a few buttons."

While I was tired of complaining, there was no way I was prepared to do the job for him. The thought of handling his smelly sports socks and sweaty basketball jerseys made me nauseous. And besides, I did more than my fair share anyway, so I insisted that he take care of his laundry himself.

That evening after dinner though, when I barged into his room looking for my iPod, the stench almost caused me to throw up.

"How can you sleep in here?" I screeched before racing to open the window.

The odor had to be caused by the pile of dirty washing dumped on the floor by his bed, along with the assortment of dirty dishes and empty take away food containers strewn across his desk.

"You're a disgrace!" I yelled as I grabbed my iPod and slammed the door shut behind me.

He was so involved in his computer game, as usual, that he completely ignored me, obviously not at all bothered by the state of his room. Thankfully, the cleaning lady was due the following day so the house would become livable again, and in particular, Matt's bedroom. If left much longer, his room would probably take on a life of its own.

Shaking my head in disgust, I trudged back towards my own room, stopping on the way to rummage through the hallway closet for my winter quilt. I had recently replaced it with a lighter one as the nights had begun to turn quite warm. But after a week of unusually warm weather, it had abruptly turned cool again.

Just as I was about to close the door, a whole pile of blankets and pillows tumbled onto the floor. With an annoyed sigh, I gathered them together and shoved them back onto the shelves they had fallen from. The cupboard was a mess, with towels, sheets and an assortment of bits and pieces haphazardly folded and stashed away. I made a mental note to tidy it up sometime.

"Unbelievable!" I muttered quietly. "What has my life come to, if I'm taking the time to worry about tidying the hallway closet?"

In my second attempt to quickly close the door, another large item toppled out and I reached for it before it hit the floor. It was my guitar case, which had been leaning against a pile of old blankets in the rear corner. Since arriving back in Carindale, I'd forgotten all about it. In fact, since middle school, I had barely touched it at all. Moving to a country property and becoming the owner of my own pony had filled every spare moment and there was no time for playing guitar.

On impulse, I pulled the case out of the cupboard, closed the door firmly before anything else could fall out and headed for my room. Sitting down on my bed, I carefully removed the guitar from its case, the feel of it in my hands creating a familiar thrill. As I strummed a few chords, I thought back to the band that Blake, Millie, a couple of others and I had once put together. We'd even won a school talent show; at that point in time, my guitar and music were so important to me.

With the guitar in my hands, I had an irresistible urge to

play it. After spending a few minutes tuning it, I turned on my laptop and went straight to YouTube to search for a song that I could strum along to. Playing guitar was such a cool thing to do and I reveled in the sounds I found myself creating. My worries and concerns melted away and quite magically, I was soon overcome with a serene feeling of peace, one that I had not experienced for a long time.

Ignoring my previous plans to do school work, I searched for the music for some of the latest hit songs and focused on mastering the chords. Before long, two hours had passed and my fingertips, unaccustomed to the constant pressure of the strings, were red raw from playing. But I'd been so captivated that I had persevered regardless.

Smiling to myself, I carefully placed my guitar back in its case and made a note of the songs I'd like to learn. Glancing back towards my computer, I realized that since I'd started playing a couple of hours earlier, I hadn't thought about Facebook at all.

With thoughts of Ky foremost in my mind, I logged on with the hope that he may have messaged me, but there were no new messages. Instantly, my happy mood faded away as I thought back to science class and wondered if his interest was simply a figment of my imagination.

I was relieved I hadn't mentioned Ky or my feelings to any of the girls at school. That would have been embarrassing, especially if he really wasn't interested. Glancing through my newsfeed, I scanned the posts with little interest and then spotted a notification. Clicking on it curiously, I discovered it was an invitation to Like a page dedicated entirely to our new English teacher.

The page was titled 'Miss Boooomley.' The name perfectly suited her booming, screeching voice and already it had several Likes. Amongst the comments were some hilarious ones that caused me to laugh out loud and I was glad for the distraction. One boy in our class, who was constantly joking around had said the funniest things, mainly mimicking the way she talked as well as her mannerisms. It was all innocent humor and without thinking too much about it, I clicked Like before shutting down the computer and finally hopping into bed.

As I switched off my bedside lamp, I thought once more of my unfinished English homework and promised myself to complete as much as possible the following night. It was due by the end of the week and I didn't want to add Miss Bromley's detention class to my list of problems.

Repercussions...

The week dragged by. Lisa continued to be very cool towards me, barely acknowledging me at all and making only occasional brief conversation. I decided to ignore her and hope she'd eventually decide to talk to me so I could convince her that dating Joe was not a good choice at all. In the meantime, I was glad to hear that her date for the weekend only involved an afternoon movie. I just hoped that was all it would amount to.

Ky was absent from our science class each day and when I searched the parking lot for his car, it was nowhere to be seen. There had been no further Facebook messages either and I began to believe I really had imagined a connection between us.

My mood soured until I reminded myself that Millie would soon be back from her overseas trip. That thought helped to cheer me up; her return simply could not come quickly enough.

At roll call on Friday morning, I was unexpectedly handed a notice to report to the conference room in the administration block. As I made my way there, I appreciated the timing which gave me a chance to skip my English class. It was definitely a lucky break to escape Miss Bromley's painful voice and boring lesson.

When I arrived at the conference room, I looked tentatively inside and discovered that a number of students were already seated around the long table. Amongst them were Lisa, Suzy and several others from our grade, each person unsure as to why they'd been summoned. It was obviously something rather important as that room was primarily reserved for meetings of the student council members and school leaders. We all waited patiently, while at the same time feeling quite special to have been selected.

To our shock and dismay though, when Mr. Fitzgerald, our deputy principal entered the room, the atmosphere immediately changed.

His presence was commanding at the best of times and every student in the school was wary of him. He was the type of person who could silence a room with a single word and that morning was no exception. As soon as he opened his mouth, his tone was full of anger causing each of us to sit up straighter in our seats.

As he spoke, my stomach lurched. The meeting was definitely not in any way positive and our smiles melted into oblivion as we focused on the angry words coming from Mr. Fitzgerald's mouth.

His face was a mask of fury as he ranted on about the appropriate use of social media and the dire consequences of posting inappropriate material online. I had no idea what he was referring to and looked blankly around the table at the others. But their eyes were darting every which way, the guilt clear on their faces.

It was then that he opened his laptop and turned the screen towards us so that we had an unobstructed view of what he was talking about. Staring back was the Facebook page, titled "Miss Boooomley" which included a very unflattering photo of a wild looking woman, probably from Google images, inserted as the profile picture. It was uncanny, I thought right then, how much that photo actually did resemble our new English teacher. But that was the last rational thought that passed through my mind as I began to process the consequences of what we were all involved in.

Throughout Mr. Fitzgerald's tirade, it was the word 'expelled' that made me really sit up and take notice. Feeling myself break into an uncomfortable sweat, I became aware of the heat which was consuming me like a wall of raging fire. Gulping for air, I looked urgently towards the nearest open window.

After clicking the Like button on that page earlier in the week, I had not given it another thought but evidently, a long list of posts and comments along with the profile picture had since been added. The inappropriateness of each was what Mr. Fitzgerald was pointing out to us. This was followed by the threat of expulsion for whoever was responsible.

I sat there envisioning the consequences of the mistake I'd made. Why on earth had I Liked that page? If only I had ignored it and moved on. Why was I always so impulsive?

My mother's familiar voice sounded in my head. As always, it happened at the most random of moments. "Think before you act, Julia!"

Shaking away thoughts of my mother as well as her reaction when she was informed, which I was sure she would be at some stage, I concentrated on Mr. Fitzgerald's words. Apparently, a similar scenario had recently occurred at a private school in the city which I vaguely recalled hearing about in the news. This particular story had gone viral and the school's reputation had suffered terribly. Apart from the fact that a teacher had been ridiculed on social media, the story had been broadcast all over the state and there had been an investigation into the school and the computer usage of the students. This, of course, was the worst possible kind of publicity and Mr. Fitzgerald wanted to avoid the same thing happening at Carindale High at all costs.

When he finally paused for breath, I glanced around the table at the others but was confronted by a look of fear on each face. We were then ordered to leave the room and told to wait outside until we were called. Mr. Fitzgerald's intention was to ask the school guidance officer to assist him in interviewing each of us individually in order to gauge our level of involvement.

Silently joining the others, I sat in the waiting area next to the office. No one dared to speak but the glances amongst the group spoke volumes. We all knew we were in serious trouble and we waited anxiously for our names to be announced.

I glanced helplessly at Lisa who instantly looked away. It was clear that she did not want me as an ally. Feeling sick to my stomach, I waited quietly with the others. A girl called Shelley was the unlucky one to be questioned first. We had no idea who would be called in after her but the minutes ticked by like a time bomb, waiting to explode.

Finally, Shelley opened the door. Ashen-faced, she stared at us and I could see that her eyes were wet with tears. Without speaking, she rushed down the hallway towards the bathroom.

I tried to breathe, deep breaths, in and out, anything to calm my nerves and staunch the sick feeling sitting heavily in my stomach. Fate had a cruel way of throwing unexpected events in my path and I wondered fleetingly what was ahead.

When eventually it was my turn to stand and face what felt like a firing squad, I thought my knees might give way and I gripped onto the chair for support. I took another deep breath before walking back into the conference room but once inside, the next few minutes passed by in a blur. Overwhelmed, the shock still vibrating through my body, I soon found myself leaving the room and making my way to the bathroom to join the others.

One glance was all I needed to realize that out of the entire group, I was the only one who had been spared. Due to the fact that after pressing the Like button, I'd had no further interaction with the Facebook page, my only consequence was a stern warning and that was all. The others were not so lucky.

Although miraculously, no one had been expelled, each person involved had been issued with instant suspensions, the length of which varied depending on the level of involvement. Shelley, who had created the page in the first place, was given the maximum penalty, a two-week suspension, and I looked on in sympathy as she held her face in her hands and cried.

Mr. Fitzgerald had informed her that along with everyone else who was suspended, the incident would be added to her school record. Her hopes for a college scholarship in the future may be in jeopardy, all because of a foolish prank.

"Why was I so stupid?" she sobbed. "It was all supposed to be just harmless fun. I never expected this to happen!"

Once again, the relief washed over me in waves. I knew my parents would receive a phone call but apart from that, the incident was over and I would be given no further consequences.

For the rest of the group though, one of the major concerns was the expected reaction from their parents, and apart from Shelley, Lisa appeared the most distraught.

"My dad will kill me," she wailed. "I'll probably be

grounded for a whole year!"

I thought of my own parents, my father in particular, who I did not want to disappoint. I knew that he wouldn't be impressed and would probably give me a huge lecture on the pros and cons of Facebook, of course mainly focusing on all the negative aspects that he could possibly think of. Although that was unnecessary, as there was no way I'd ever be involved in anything of the kind again.

"I bet someone dobbed us in!" moaned Shelley staring angrily at the others. "Miss Bromley probably doesn't even use Facebook. She would never have known if someone hadn't dobbed!"

"It would have been one of those nerds who love to suck up!" one of the others added angrily, "Someone hoping to get on her good side; anything for a decent mark!"

"Oh no!!!" Lisa stammered. "I've just realized something!"

"What?" Shelley prompted. "What's wrong now?"

"I'll be grounded for sure and now I won't be able to go to the movies with Joe tomorrow!"

To Lisa, this was the worst consequence of all. The look of devastation on her face overtook everything else and instantly she burst into tears.

Anxiously, I looked on, not knowing what to say; although, I considered her punishment a blessing in disguise and was convinced that being unable to make her date was the best thing that could have happened to her.

As far as any serious repercussions though, I'd been spared. It was clear that no one else had been so lucky and I didn't dare make any comments of my own. I also knew that my sympathy would not be appreciated.

In order to escape any further upset, especially with Lisa, I decided to make a quick exit.

Feeling a mixture of empathy for the others and complete relief for myself, I hurried to my next class. Extremely grateful that first period was over and I was able to avoid Miss Bromley, I walked down the hallway towards the science labs.

Just as I reached the classroom door, I came face to face with Ky.

Roller Coaster...

He had appeared from the opposite direction. I had my head down, deep in thought, still reeling with emotion over the morning's events. When I looked up, there he was, approaching the doorway at the exact same moment.

Our eyes connected and I felt a small thrill as a shiver ran quickly down my spine.

"Hey," I said shyly, as I entered the room.

"Hey," he replied, his brown eyes staring into mine.

My heart thumping, I walked towards the back and sat down in the first vacant spot I could find. Coincidentally, there happened to be a spare seat next to mine and I glanced at it as I placed my books on the benchtop in front of me.

Barely daring to breathe, I kept my eyes on the teacher at the front of the room, while watching in my peripheral vision as Ky sat down alongside me.

"Okay if I sit here?" he whispered quietly, not wanting to draw any further attention our way.

We had both arrived a few minutes late and had already been given a stern look by Mr. Anderson, our teacher.

"Yeah, that's fine," I replied with a nervous smile.

I didn't dare to glance at Ky again. But my whole body was tingling and it was as though a current of sparking electricity was passing directly between us.

I tried to focus my attention on Mr. Anderson, who was in

the midst of revising everything we'd already learned during the semester. It was in preparation for an exam the following week but I was barely able to concentrate on what he was saying. I don't think I comprehended a word.

Throughout the majority of the lesson, my conscious mind was only on the boy sitting next to me and although I took no obvious notice of him, I was overcome by his presence.

Sneaking an occasional glance from the corner of my eye, I watched his hand as it held tightly to a pen and wrote down the notes from the board…long fingers, olive skin and a ring on his left index finger. It was a narrow band, silver in color, and from my vantage point, it appeared to be engraved with some sort of symbol.

He was left-handed, I noticed; such an unusual trait. I didn't think I knew anyone who was left-handed, not personally anyway. My lips twitched at the corners as I wondered if I'd ever get to know him personally.

Fate was such a strange thing. If I hadn't been through the Facebook ordeal which caused me to be late to class, I may not have had the chance to sit next to him. It may never have happened. But was all this going to lead anywhere? That was the question.

Momentarily, Blake's face flashed into my mind. Why did thoughts of him so often appear? And at the most unpredictable of moments! Would I forever be haunted by his existence?

Forcing myself to get a grip on reality and the fact that I really needed to be focusing on the lesson, I scribbled notes from the board onto my notepad, anything to look busy. Although when I later attempted to read through them, I could barely decipher the scrawl.

It was crazy. There I was in a crucial science revision lesson and all I could concentrate on were boys, in particular, the one sitting right beside me.

A few minutes later, when his knee brushed against my own, I was forced to smother the gasp that threatened to escape my lips. Pretending a cough, I wondered if it had been accidental. Or had he intentionally allowed his leg to touch mine? I didn't dare move, but sat rigid, concentrating on trying to control the electric currents racing through my body.

It was so strange. A person I hardly knew was having the most intense effect on me, and I wondered if he had any inclination at all of what I was feeling.

When I glanced at the clock on the wall and realized the lesson was almost over, I felt a rush of panic. What should I do? Be friendly? Say something? Although I had no idea what! Or should I just try to act cool, not speak at all, simply get up and leave?

Class was about to end and I was so concerned that I would ruin the moment; lose the perfect opportunity to at least strike up a conversation. As if in answer to my prayer, the solution was handed to me, without any effort on my part at all.

Everyone stood to move out into the hallway, eager to get to morning recess. As Ky and I had been sitting towards the back, we were among the last to leave.

I searched for something interesting to say to him; anything to get his attention. Then I heard the teacher's voice. "Julia. Ky. Would you guys mind giving me a hand, please? I need some help to carry this pile of books down to the storeroom."

"Oh, sure, Mr. Anderson," Ky responded without any hesitation at all. Glancing at me, his intense gaze bored deep into my soul.

"Err, that's fine, Mr. Anderson," I added, my pulse spiking at the idea of spending another five minutes at Ky's side.

To my utter delight, those five minutes became another twenty, as one trip to the storeroom resulted in several. I could not think of another way that I'd rather spend my morning break. By the time we had finished, Ky and I were laughing and joking and I was finally feeling more at ease in his company.

That was until our work was done, then all of a sudden, we were left standing alone together in the hallway. It was one of those awkward moments where one stares at the other and each person is at a loss for what to say.

Fearful of embarrassing myself, I took sideways glances, while frantically trying to find the right words. I was mute, unable to speak and felt a red blush creep over my skin as I waited for him to say something, anything at all to camouflage the intensity of the moment.

My heart was pounding in my chest but I was unable to move. It was a weird sensation because I really didn't know quite what to do. His penetrating brown eyes stared into mine and then, at the same time, we both opened our mouths to speak.

"Sorry," I smiled. "You first."

And then he murmured the words I had been hoping to hear.

"Do you want to hang out sometime?"

Just as I was about to reply, the bell to resume classes

clanged in our ears, and I grinned at him as I waited for the deafening noise to end.

Eventually, the sound stopped and I found the courage to respond to his question. "That'd be really fun."

I looked into his eyes once again; dark pools of emotion staring back. Within seconds, the hallway was filled with gossiping students rushing to their next class, and the moment between us faded away.

Just before turning in the opposite direction, he spoke again. Three words, that was all. "I'll message you."

Then, caught up in the wave of rushing students, he was gone.

Hugging my arms close to myself as if in a silent celebratory cheer, the smile on my face rapidly spread from one side to the other. If anyone had warned me that my day would be filled with a roller coaster of emotions which included shock and despair and then unexpectedly turn into outright joy, I would never have believed them.

I soon discovered though, the craziness of my day was far from over.

Chaos...

In the middle of our math lesson, a piercing siren suddenly blasted the airwaves. It was an unrelenting noise that made me cringe. I caught the look of panic on our substitute teacher who had never taught at Carindale High before and was at a loss for what to do.

At first, we all assumed it was a fire drill. These happened on a regular basis and while the teachers found them frustrating because lessons were interrupted, the students were happy for an excuse to waste time and escape from class.

"It's a fire alarm, Miss!" Jack, one of the boys who was seated at the front of the room explained.

Most kids were already on their feet. Our usual procedure was to make our way outside and assemble with the rest of the school on the sports field, which was situated away from all the buildings.

The teacher was clearly flustered and insisted that everyone remain in their seats until she was able to call the office and confirm what was happening. Several kids ignored her and continued towards the door whilst others took advantage of some free time to chat with their friends.

The noise level in the room quickly reached maximum volume with everyone raising their voices in order to be heard above the din. Meanwhile, the teacher attempted to listen to the voice on the other end of the phone.

In the abrupt blink of an eye, the chaos in the room was silenced by her words, *"ITS A LOCKDOWN!!!"*

Immediately, all heads turned towards the panicked voice that was yelling at us from across the room. The teacher's obvious distress was all the proof we needed. It was not a regular drill; we really did have a genuine lockdown occurring in our school.

I had never experienced anything other than practice sessions before and it seemed that this was the case with everyone else in the room, including the teacher.

After rushing to lock the door, she began yelling at us to get under the desks and stay down. Several kids automatically obeyed her while others looked around in confusion.

Amidst the bedlam, we heard someone yell, *"OMG! WHAT'S GOING ON??"*

It was then that the distinct sound of shattering glass and wild commotion right outside the windows caught the attention of every person in the room. Several kids crouched below the row of large windows that lined the wall and peered out. I dared to join them and instantly caught a frightening glimpse of the danger that we should have been hiding from.

Out of nowhere, appeared a senior student, his crazed expression betraying his unbalanced state of mind. I recognized him immediately by the large stretchers in his ears. This was a standout feature that had caught my attention on several occasions throughout the semester. I had stared in fascination at the huge holes in his earlobes, although I later learned that piercings such as these were against school rules.

At that moment though, it wasn't the stretchers in his ears that were the issue. Rather, it was the glint of the large knife blade, the handle of which he gripped tightly as he wielded it in a wide arc in the air around him. The demented look in his eyes as he swung the knife, ready to attack anyone who dared to confront him was the scariest part. When he turned towards our window and saw us staring fearfully in his direction, I heard several petrified screams behind me.

Some kids remained standing, transfixed with fear until they finally registered the sound of the teacher's voice.

"Get under the desks!" she yelled, the hysteria rising in her throat. "MOVE! NOW!!"

Rapidly, I joined the others who scrambled for cover; anywhere to hide from the deranged pair of eyes glaring our way.

Squeals of fear continued around me, while our teacher called for us to be quiet. Though we had already been spotted and I couldn't understand the logic of remaining in the room within view.

Crawling under the nearest desk, I waited for instructions. Then, when I happened to look behind me, I stared into the eyes of Sara Hamilton.

Her contorted features as she scowled back were clearly not due to the danger lurking outside the classroom windows. Instinctively, I knew her expression was directed at me and I couldn't believe that I was crouched under a desk next to the one person I most wanted to avoid.

I considered moving to another spot, but the teacher had already warned everyone to stay put. Although the figure of the boy outside was no longer in view, the room remained thick with fear.

Soft moans and sobs could be heard around the room, but they quickly turned to sharp screams at the sound of more smashing glass just outside.

Several heads popped up and a few boys rushed to the windows, eager to see what had caused the noise. This was met with more yelling from our teacher, who was frantically trying to maintain control.

At the sound of even more shattering glass, I heard Sara gasp and then felt her sudden grip on my arm. It was obviously an involuntary reaction caused by the noise outside. I recalled having once done the exact same thing myself during a scary scene at the cinema where I grabbed hold of the man sitting next to me. It was incredibly embarrassing, especially because he was a complete stranger.

Sara frowned as she pulled her hand away and I wondered vaguely whether she might also feel embarrassed. But there was much more to worry about than Sara embarrassing herself.

The muffled cries of several frightened kids caught my attention.

"Where's he gone?"

What's going on out there?"

"Is he going to attack us with that knife?"

"OMG! We're going to die!!!"

"Just keep your voices down and stay where you are. We'll be okay." With a wavering voice, the teacher attempted to calm the panic that was erupting around her. But her words did little to reassure us.

We heard angry shouts followed by a loud ruckus. A few boys rushed to the windows and Jack called out excitedly, "It's the police!"

Within seconds, just about every student in the room ran to the windows or climbed on top of desks to get a better view. The teacher yelled at us to get down and stay hidden but her words fell on deaf ears. The excitement outside was too much and we watched, mesmerized, as the policemen tackled the boy to the ground. He fought furiously, lashing out with his feet and fists in an attempt to escape. Thankfully at that stage, the knife had been tossed onto the grass a safe distance away.

Behind us, the teacher yelled for everyone to stay away from the windows but she had no hope at all of maintaining any sort of order.

We watched the police handcuff the boy and drag him to his feet. Our entire class was overcome with emotion and this ranged from tears and sobs to loud cheering, as the boy was led towards the nearby police van.

A few girls remained cowering at the back of the classroom. The whole episode had been extremely frightening and my heart was still hammering in my chest as the police van drove out of the parking lot and disappeared down the road.

Later that night, I recounted the entire incident to Matt, right from the moment we heard the lockdown siren blasting throughout the school. He listened with envy to the details, frustrated that he was confined to his classroom on the other side of the campus with no idea what was going on.

However, he did have some background information to share. Apparently, the boy had been expelled from other schools previously, and often arrived late to class with glassy eyes and looking pretty spaced out. It was obvious that he was into drugs of some sort and for whatever reason, he'd lost control. As to what caused the rampage, we had no idea.

I then went on to tell Matt about the Facebook drama. Once again, he sat riveted while I gave him all the details. As Miss Bromley also taught his English class, he thought the FB page in her honor was extremely funny, in particular, some of the posts and comments that had been added as they described her perfectly.

But as soon as he heard the consequences handed out by our deputy principal, he quickly changed his reaction. The idea of Mr. Fitzgerald exploding in our faces as he ranted and raved about the inappropriateness of what we had done, followed by suspension for most of the people involved, was enough to discourage Matt from ever considering something similar.

Glancing at the clock on the kitchen wall, I saw the time had flown by. I couldn't remember ever connecting so well with my brother before and definitely not talking with him for so long. Usually, after we'd finished eating dinner and had cleaned up the kitchen, he rushed back to his computer while I retreated to my own little world within my bedroom.

I looked at him affectionately and thought back to the days not so long ago when he constantly annoyed me. At times, I couldn't stand him near me and would be bothered by his presence in the same room. But somehow, along the way, that feeling had changed and I now looked at him in a completely different light.

It occurred to me also, that he had become very good looking and I sat admiring the way his wavy blond hair swept across his forehead.

Flicking it out of his eyes, he grinned cheekily. He really was the most likable person and had such a fun personality. These traits, combined with his good looks made him a popular target for girls. Lately, he was swamped with interest from several different girls not only from his own grade but from other schools as well. I often had difficulty keeping up with all the names of the girls he talked about, although interestingly enough, at the moment, he didn't have a steady girlfriend.

One detail I didn't mention to him was my crush on Ky. That was something I preferred to keep to myself.

Since arriving home that afternoon, I had constantly kept a check on Facebook hoping to find the message Ky had promised, but apart from a quick hi from Millie, there were no other messages at all.

I thought again of Ky's words earlier that day and repeated them in my head. *Do you want to hang out sometime?* The image of his smiling face created an instant thrill inside me.

Filled with anxious anticipation over what might lie ahead, I followed Matt up the stairs and quickly checked my messages once more. When the blank message icon appeared on the screen, the disappointment was almost too much and I slumped back on my bed, wondering again if I was creating something out of nothing.

Feeling drained from the tension of the day, I closed my laptop and decided to get ready for bed. Knowing that I'd see Ky at school the following day, I attempted to shut out all negative thoughts.

Within seconds of my head hitting the pillow, I was in a deep sleep, oblivious to what was in store for me next.

Whirlwind...

Quickly grabbing a pile of books from my locker, I was panicky with the realization that if I didn't hurry, I'd be late for my English class. I was sure that after the Facebook incident I was already on Miss Bromley's radar and did not want to give her any further reasons to notice me.

Looking around as I banged my locker door closed, I noted Sara rummaging through her own locker only a few meters away. I had thought it so unfortunate to have a locker situated close to hers and at one stage requested a new one in a different location. But unfortunately, there were none available.

Tilting my head sideways in order to allow my long hair to drape over my face like a veil, I glanced discreetly towards her from the corner of one eye. I didn't want to attract her attention but I was struck by something unusual and was keen to get a better look.

She must have sensed me staring because she flicked her flowing blond hair behind her shoulder and turned sharply towards me.

The expression on her face was a mixture of arrogance and scorn. "What are you looking at?"

Ignoring her rude retort, I took a step past her but made sure to keep my eyes focused ahead of me. She was clearly in a foul mood and I didn't want to risk upsetting her further. Not that it took much to upset that girl. I had heard her angry outburst towards a junior student just the day before when she had accidentally bumped into Sara in the hallway.

But in my haste to pass by, I dropped one of my books on the floor. When I bent down to pick it up, everything else I was holding slipped from my grasp as well. My entire body flushed with heat as I crouched down in an attempt to gather the items together. I lifted my gaze ever so slightly and saw that Sara remained steadfast in her position, watching my every move.

She was obviously enjoying my humiliation and kept her eyes focused on my crouched figure, delighting in the fact that her presence was adding to my discomfort. When I stood upright, my pile of books and bits and pieces haphazardly collected in my arms, I attempted to once again step around her, but to my dismay, she side-stepped in front of me, blocking my path.

Forced to make eye contact, I looked at her with raised eyebrows and a slight shake of my head. I was determined not to let her get to me and resisted the temptation to voice the words that filled my thoughts.

I wanted to let her have it, to call her every name I could think of. But I was well aware that I'd be stooping to her level and encouraging further harassment. So I gathered all the strength I could and kept my mouth firmly closed.

Smirking obnoxiously, she continued to stare as I stepped past her. I could feel her eyes burning into my back but I kept my head tall and forced myself to walk on. I was sure she'd been hoping for a reaction but I refused to give her the pleasure. Mingling with the throng of students in the hallway, I was eager to be as far away from her as possible.

I tried without success to focus on Miss Bromley's boring monologue. I just couldn't shake the vision of my encounter with Sara. Apart from her evil glare, what struck me so vividly was her noticeable loss of weight. I had been well aware that she'd lost weight when I last saw her, but she now appeared to be even thinner.

It was certainly a surprise to see her clothes hanging loosely from her tiny frame. She had always had such an amazing body, she looked fantastic in anything she wore and I was unable to believe the dramatic change.

The word anorexia entered my mind and I wondered if that was her problem. Why she would feel the need to lose weight was beyond me. I had read that anorexic people considered themselves overweight even if they weren't, and wondered if that were the case with Sara. Apparently, it was a psychological illness that a huge number of young people suffered from, worldwide. Although I had never personally known anyone with the condition, I was fairly certain that it must describe Sara.

Switching my thoughts entirely, I considered the fact that I still hadn't heard from Ky. From my seat, I had a clear view of the student parking lot and I glanced out the window, figuring that I could at least determine if he were at school or not. When I failed to spot his car, I sighed with disappointment.

Deciding that I needed to be patient, I looked towards the board and tried to absorb the words displayed there. We'd been given a passage from Shakespeare to analyze and were expected to interpret the symbolism depicted throughout. The text made no sense to me and I found it very difficult to comprehend what Miss Bromley was talking about.

Shakespeare was supposed to be a senior topic anyway, and we had all complained when she admitted that it was not part of the curriculum for our year level. Her argument was that if we spent some time focusing on that genre during one of our junior semesters, it would introduce us to the topic in question and prepare us for our senior grades.

"OMG, she's unbelievable!" I heard the muttering behind me and gave a nod of agreement.

Finally, though, the bell clanged loudly and we could escape. A double period of English was absolute torture and I sighed with relief when the lesson was over. Heading outside for morning break, I looked towards the spot where I usually sat with the other girls and could see them chatting animatedly. As I drew nearer, I heard Beth's excited voice and wondered what new gossip had them all so captivated.

"What's going on?" I asked curiously as I approached.

Suzy looked at me, wide-eyed. "Have you heard the latest, Julia? About Blake Jansen and Monica Peterson?"

Instantly my stomach dropped.

"No," I replied. "I don't think I have."

"They're the latest hot couple and apparently Sara is furious!" Becky, the girl alongside Suzy, who I'd noticed always wore the coolest clothes, added.

"Yeah," Beth smirked, "That's probably why she's so skinny now! That's my guess anyway!"

I looked from one girl to the other, speechless and in shock.

Blake and Monica? Monica, the pretty girl who I had seen him hanging out with so often lately?

I considered the fact that just the other day, I'd caught the two of them deep in conversation and fits of laughter, totally comfortable in each other's company. I had looked on, unnoticed, while familiar jealous pangs wormed their way into the depths of my being; just like the cruel blow of a blunt ax hacking mercilessly, with absolutely no regard for the damage being inflicted.

My mind reeled in confusion as I tried to comprehend what Beth was saying.

Had he really moved on to someone else? Had it actually become official? Was it not something I had simply imagined amidst my fits of silent envy?

Shaking my head in disbelief, I sat quietly while the girls continued to gossip about the latest new hook-ups and romances that had recently developed amongst the students in our grade.

I tried to come to terms with this new turn of events and also to take control of the whirlwind in my mind and soul.

But why was I so concerned? Wasn't I the one who was convinced it couldn't work between us? And wasn't I the one who had decided to move on?

I felt nauseous, the bile rising in my throat. It wasn't fair. If I couldn't have him, I wanted no-one else to either.

The hardest part was that I was aware, completely aware that I had no right to feel this way. He'd tried; several times he had tried. But I had simply brushed him away, too proud to return his feelings after he betrayed me with Sara. Although, deep inside my heart, all I wanted was for us to be together again.

Looking up, I spotted a familiar figure heading towards me.

Staring in his direction, confused thoughts raced through my mind.

As he approached and our eyes connected, I watched the

warm smile appear on his face.

"Hi, Julia!" his smooth voice caught the attention of all the girls around me, who abruptly stopped their conversation to stare at him, the interest and curiosity clearly evident in their expressions.

Stunned and totally confused, I replied, "Hello, Ky."

My eyes locked on his as he sat down beside me.

***

Find out what happens next in

Julia Jones – The Teenage Years - Book 3: True Love

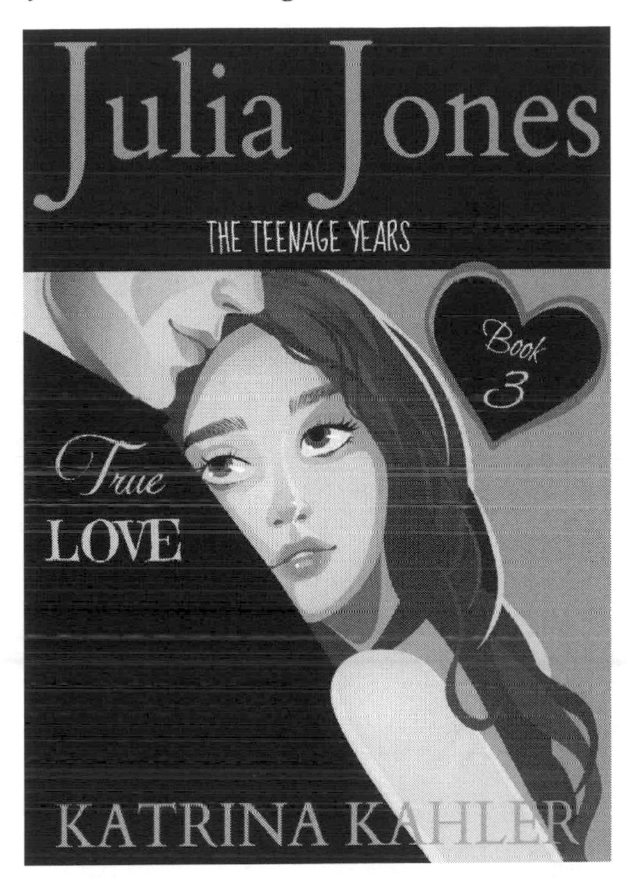

Follow Julia Jones on Instagram @juliajonesdiary

Please Like our Facebook page

to keep updated on the release date for each new book in the series…

Facebook.com/JuliaJonesDiary

Have you read the prequel to this series yet?

Julia Jones' Diary is a best seller – great for girls 9 – 13 and young teens as well!

Julia Jones' Diary – My Worst Day Ever!

Here are some more fabulous books for girls that you're sure to enjoy…

Mind Reader – Book 1: My New Life

This story continues on from Julia Jones' Diary and features Julia Jones, Millie, Sara, and Blake - it follows the story of Julia and her friends after Julia left for the country.

It's another very popular book for girls.

The Lost Girl
Bella's Story
Book 1
Katrina Kahler
Twins
Book 1
Swapped
Katrina Kahler

Time Traveler
The Discovery
Book 1
Katrina Kahler
Mean Girls
My New Step-Sister
Book 1
Katrina Kahler
Charlotte Birch

35141059R00057

Made in the USA
Lexington, KY
01 April 2019